D1602341

ALL

THE

Stories & Poetry

WOODS

SHE

Emily McCosh

WATCHES

OVER

OCEANS IN
· THE SKY ·

Cover design, illustrations, and formatting by Emily McCosh
Edited by Natalia Leigh (Enchanted Ink Publishing)

Published by Oceans In The Sky Press
OceansInTheSky.com

OCEANS IN
·THE SKY·

Love you Mom & Dad

PRAISE FOR
ALL THE WOODS SHE WATCHES OVER

"A captivating collection that puts an inventive spin on fantasy and sci-fi while wrapping itself around your heart. *All The Woods She Watches Over* is a treasure, and I eagerly await more from Emily McCosh."

— Jenna Moreci, #1 Bestseller of *The Savior's Champion*

"This delightful collection of sometimes sweet and sometimes painful stories show us what it is to be human, albeit not always through human eyes. A true talent to keep on your radar."

— William Ledbetter, Bestselling Author of *Level Five*

"Heartwarming and heart-wrenching, beautiful and magical and strange, and all-around spellbinding."

— Natalia Leigh, Author of *Pistol Daisy*

Only the keeper sees

That, where the ring-dove broods,

And the badgers roll at ease,

There was once a road through the woods.

— Rudyard Kipling,

"The Way Through the Woods"

CONTENTS

Our Wired Hearts I

Breath, Weeping Wind, Death 9

Robot Dreams 17

We Are Not Faerytales 37

The Stars and the Rain 45

Of Water and Wood 53

Frozen Meadow, Shining Sun 63

Cookies for Ghost 85

Get Down 91

The Petals on Her Lips 97

Paper Found in Garden,
Secured with Locket, Unbroken 107

All the Woods She Watches Over 113

Acknowledgments 137

About the Author 139

Publication History 141

OUR WIRED HEARTS

He's the first I've seen with flesh fused in his metal hands, and he's repairing violins outside a corner shop. The music store leans against the café that I've frequented since returning from the war. I imagine him in the back room, polishing wood, tuning pianos, stringing guitars. Hiding from daylight.

Sunlight glints off the metal in his hands, the wired ligaments and tendons, brightening the pale strips of skin woven throughout. When I stop, he looks me up and down in a way that says he hasn't met a person of plastic, wire, and metal since coming home.

"Sky or land?" I ask without approaching. We all fought somewhere. We all had to find a place to live in peace when it was over.

He points skyward.

"If I buy you a coffee sometime, will you play for me?" We can eat and drink for social occasions, and it sounds like a human question.

I've made a religion of never approaching my own kind,

of never reminding myself that I was created to be a soldier then scrapped parts. But I want to hear music. Not the kind on radio or in a bar. If I had a childhood, I'd say I was looking for nostalgia.

For not speaking a word, his smile speaks volumes.

. . .

His name is Andrew, and he discovers that I dance in the theater two streets down. Once, he's in the park just outside when I leave; eyes closed; playing the violin with a soldier's passion. Only the pigeons pay him mind, crowding his feet in fluid movements, looking for a hand to feed them. People give him passing glances without smiling and never stop to listen. We are relics of a recent human past they're eager to forget, walking among them like ghosts, artificial and unreal.

I watch from the theater. I've avoided him since requesting he play for me, not wishing to be around a metal man who turns himself to flesh. We are not human, not made to feel and interact. We shouldn't pretend.

I almost leave. With his tin eyelids closed, I could sneak past on quiet feet. Still, I like the way his skin looks in the light. The way his face, robotic as mine, expresses iron emotion.

I let him find me here, sitting where other people ignore us, and buy him a coffee.

. . .

His voicebox is broken, and he has little money, not enough to fix it. It was not caused by firefight or bomb, but by a bus soon after he returned home. The driver was exhausted.

Asleep at the wheel.

Andrew makes signs with his metal-and-skin hands. He teaches me to understand some of them until I feel as if we're speaking a language all our own. He says the bus is ironic. I would call it a tragedy, but I think that would insult his smile.

. . .

In the park—our favorite place, him away from a boss that gives him the side-eye, me away from the other dancers who expect me to be either wholly human and emotional or utterly metal and heartless—he tries to teach me the violin. My metal fingers are not so graceful as my feet. The sound they make is heavy, unpleasant, and entirely wrong. Perhaps he's wise to have flesh in his. The thought is something else entirely. I don't realize I've ceased playing until he uses those hands to readjust my grip on the violin bow.

"I have no talent," I tell him, and he laughs without a voice and with all the joy.

Talent is optional, his fingers say. *Passion is key.*

I manage three decent notes before he asks, *Dance for me?*

I take off my boots and arch my cool feet in the grass.

. . .

"Why?" I ask the first time I touch the veins of skin in his hands and arms. We're sitting in the park where flowering raspberry bushes hide us and trees offer shade. I lay his palms along my legs and measure the length of my fingers beside his.

It isn't true skin, not by human standards. That would require a beating heart with thrumming veins and microscopic rivers of blood through every inch of him. It's synthetic, invented to heal the frail bodies of humans. But it is—unlike the rest of us—soft, warm, and breakable. Every bit of it: unique. It is as close to alive as we'll ever be.

The only distinction between my own fingers are the notches left by the work of war. His are the same, but the fragile skin bears pale scars and calluses left by violin strings.

How strange I thought it was before—how unnatural to pretend we are real. He seems very real to me.

To feel when I play. He turns my palms over, placing his atop mine. *It makes the emotions stronger.*

"Flesh is so much more breakable. It's frail."

He gives me the all-expressive smile. *But it feels the best in our wired hearts.*

· · ·

No one quite knows what allows us to feel. They say we shouldn't—the humans who made us—but we are not purely the machines we were created to be. We cannot hunger, thirst, sicken, make love or grow old. Yet I despair when people hate me. I am joyful when I dance. I feared when asking Andrew to play his music and when I saw him in the park waiting for me.

I feel rage when I go to his apartment to find pieces of him scattered on the floor, hands dripping the filmy fluid in his skin. We won humans their war and look the other way when they ignore us. Not all leave us be, and no one would bother to stop them. When I ask, he won't tell me who committed the act.

Fear is an easy emotion.

Putting him back together fills me with the urge to scream and to cry, but I can't shed tears either. I repaired dozens of my kind when I stood on the battlefield, but none I felt for. None whose despair seeped into my heart. I am helpless when cradling his hands in mine, and use ripped cloth from an old shirt to bind his skin back together. He hasn't looked at me all night.

"Andrew," I say, and for the first time his eyes look like he's never left the fight. When I kiss his temple, there's nothing but the clink of my plastic lips on his metal skull. I shift his cheekbone back into place and wish I could make him smile.

. . .

I feel an aching, bittersweet strangeness when, later that night, we lie side by side on the floor of his apartment. Staring at nothing but the darkness of the ceiling, I tell him story after story of everything I can remember since waking in the factory that created me, until his arm snakes under my head and his breath whispers butterfly patterns over my ear.

When I've run out of life to tell, we lie in silence with our arms intertwined. Feeling.

. . .

It is not his words that convince me to match his skin, nor any of the little speeches he signs about passion and art and becoming more human. Not even the pain in his expression for days after I put him back together, and the weight of his smile the morning after I lie beside him through the night. It is instead a strange longing to understand what makes him who he is. To be something other than what people see when they look at my metal shell.

The technology is good, the healing quick. The other girls

at the theater don't notice what I've done to my hands—they're staring at the shimmering metal of my feet, the still-raw skin of my toes, the soles and tops of my feet, the soft flesh running up my legs like rivers cutting a desert.

My burning muscles need training, but my mind remembers the movements and the passion.

Andrew's awe is perfect, the sun shimmering off his lips, his cheeks, his eyes. He kneels before me where I sit in the grass. His palms press to the soft soles of my feet. It's the first time he touches my fingers and feels something besides iron and wire. His entire body shakes, and I'm starting to hear music every time he laughs that silent, joyful laugh.

When he plays his violin for me, his hands finally beginning to heal, I dance in the grass with warm, bare feet.

DAPPLED

afternoon makes
his last dandelion noise
minutes before
sunset finds the horizon

when time forgets
to write his letters,
opal clouds draw
surrender flags by memory
and pinecones crack
with autumn desire

there will come a time
when humans are
faerytales and magic
roams the land in whispers

when tales are written in
the language of rabbits,
soon this dryad will shed
her bark in crumpled sheets
of history books, dappled
in the leaves of cottonwoods

it is too early for even the
birds to know how to sing lullabies,
racing in a whisper of wings between
the sun and the stars

one day soon even the flowers
will abandon their meadow

BREATH, WEEPING WIND, DEATH

There is someone watching you, and what an unfamiliar sensation that is. When was the last time you let someone take in the sight of you? Not anywhere close to here atop this New York skyscraper. And not anyone with life still in them. Only the dying do you speak to, and on occasion, the very old or very young, like this one.

It's a little girl. You can tell she thinks she's sneaky, the way she crouches behind the flowerpot—the one, large speck of greenery adorning the rooftop—folding her adolescent limbs into a ball, peeking through the fern fronds. Eyes. She has eyes like a horse. Not in appearance, but effect. Curious and heavy-lidded, looking right into your soul and calming you. Very pretty.

She doesn't *look* afraid. Then again, you're very much a man at the moment.

Don't talk to her. You know better. Don't talk to the ones you don't take with you. Leave, or at the very least, keep yourself quiet. You don't even know why she's up here.

Still, you find yourself asking, "What are you looking at, child?"

Her face disappears from between the fronds, abashed at being caught. Her voice reaches your ears muffled. "Who are you?"

You close your eyes, resting against the small cement wall of the apartment building roof. You've been sitting here so long the cold seeps into your bones. You haven't felt cold for so long, and with the wind howling, sounding too much like weeping, her question makes you tired.

"Are you supposed to talk to strangers?"

Given her age, maybe ten or eleven years, it's a question you can ask.

"You were talking to Grandma."

You look again. She's peeking around the dirty pot, hair caught in the fern, eyes wary. You can't tell what color they are in the darkness—brown, you think, or maybe black. The skin around those eyes is thin and moth-wing delicate. Red like blush, even against her dark skin, but you've seen enough of tears to know it is that and nothing else. Your heart aches. Shame makes a nest in your chest, and you don't even know if she realizes who you are.

Lying won't do you any good.

"Who do you think I am?"

She stares, frowns, and finally ignores your question. "Why were you talking to her?"

You've closed your eyes again. Your thoughts are a bat-tleground, trying to decide if she knows who you are or she's being a child talking to a stranger. It isn't as if one comes upon Death every day as an old man wearing a Darth Vader T-shirt and ragged army boots. "Because she wanted to talk."

Somehow, that brings her out. The patter of feet announces her, and her baggy blue jeans scratch as she sits mere feet away. Her presence is warm, a lamp through fog; not physical heat, but a sensation in your chest. Contentment, but different. You shudder. Every fiber of your existence is telling you that her time is far from running out.

"What did she say?" she asks.

You're honest again, although you're starting to believe you should have left the moment you noticed her sneaking. "You made her happy. She said you came up here on the roof for months and painted the city, and it was so beautiful that it won an art competition at your school. None of the other children even came close. It made her so proud."

There were other things the old woman said, gripping your hand and staring out the window. You always give them a chance to talk, to tell their secrets. It's a comfort for some. Because you're not there to judge. Just to help, really, a guiding hand between here and there. You're full of stories you've heard, bursting at the seams with them. But the rest were not confessions this child needs to know.

For a moment you're sure she's crying. She *should* be after a story like that. The bottom lip is puffed out, trembling, but she chews on it. Maybe all the tears have run out—it wouldn't be the first time. She's thinking now, pressing and folding her fingers, staring at nothing. "Mama says people just run out of time. That everyone has a time when they're supposed to"—her head cocks, almost like a wince—"die. I keep imagining a bunch of watches hanging from a ceiling. Like that *Alice in Wonderland* movie. But it's not like that, is it?"

There's a genuine tightness in your chest. You wonder if

it comes from the body you're in or that you've never been asked outright.

"No, it's nothing like that. That's people making things romantic. It's just a feeling. Like when you know someone's watching you but you turn around and no one's there. Or a bit of warmth for no reason. It's different all the time, but the same. Then I know."

The silence hurts, and you don't want to look at her. There are others who need you now; you can feel them, little throbbing pinpricks in your chest. Maybe if you left, you wouldn't be so cold. But you're tired—you don't know how it's possible to be tired of your own nature, but you feel it. You thought sitting here for a while, just taking a rest, would somehow make it better. Silly thoughts.

"You took her with you."

You've never heard such a tone from a child. Sad, but not angry. Like she just wants to make sure it's okay.

"Yes."

"Then why are you sad?"

You aren't certain, but you have an idea. "Because sometimes things that are supposed to happen can still be sad."

She looks at you for a second, chin resting on her knees, scraping her sneakers back and forth on the concrete roof. When she gets up she's ungainly, like she hasn't grown into herself. She takes the door from the roof without a word or a glance over the shoulder. You sigh, unsure if you've hurt or helped. People know of you, and you've been recognized before, talked to, but you've never talked in return, and you can't remember the last time someone didn't hate you. Funny that it came from a child.

The door creaks, and her eyes reappear. When she retakes her seat beside you, she offers the plate she's holding and sniffles.

"Grandma would say, 'Cookies help everything but your hips.'"

You chuckle, a noise that's barely there over the wind. The cookie is soft in your fingers, crumbling against your shirt, and you watch the little girl eat hers. There's no sound up here but the wind and her slow, calming breaths. She doesn't smile but sits closer, like you aren't a stranger and bringer of the end. And after a time, she talks. It's nothing important, really. She talks about the stars, and she talks about paint, and clothes, and friends, and books, and the moon. You sit, and eat, and let everything in the world act like it's okay.

And that, more than anything, makes you feel warm again.

WHEN THE DOGWOODS DANCED

i found the sun

speaking tongue twisters

with the planets

about how seasons affect little

mice and a neighboring star is

blue, blue, blue like ice under fire

in the melting of spring

how she is suspended

in darkness, and now

his fiery fingers will not

brush her butterscotch skin

for stars do not meet when

pinwheeling galaxies collide

the dogwoods danced a dream-

filled ballet with the wind,

the creek its passionate orchestra

and an audience of fireflies

accompanying the stars

i prayed the sun would

forget how to rise

because

look

sometimes the light of magic

hides in darkness

there is a creature i caught under

the pond lilies, speaking

a sun language and dancing

through the night

its heart bled ink onto my

fingers, wrapped the

wounds in paper,

telling me

see

words are

not magic

just

truth

ROBOT DREAMS

My dreams are dusk and cornfields. Long shadows and swathes of leaves crisped by the sun. Tilled lands and peach trees. Faces that may be important had I a memory to speak of. I don't believe they're real. My waking hours are four walls and a tractor-part shop to keep clean.

No, I don't believe they're real, but they overtake my powered-down thoughts.

. . .

The father I dreamt of was furious.

I'd learned his name was Jonas, a farmer of corn and potatoes, whose neighbor owned a baseball field, hedged by cornstalks, where all the children played. Jonas and his family were as poor as the soil they tilled, and his boys were too little to help.

And I wasn't what Jonas expected. I wasn't a working bot.

A man sold me. A face I don't remember. He lied in the same breath he used to thank the father for his payment. Robots weren't made anymore, and functioning ones were rare and often useless when found. The stranger who owned me took me from an old factory, offering too good a price.

Defective. Defective was the word Jonas used. I didn't understand the meaning, only the implication. I wasn't *correct*. Jonas couldn't know how useless I was, and the stranger who sold me had *lied*. Farming equipment was foreign. I had no knowledge of soil and plants and living things. I stared at the tractor Jonas placed me before, wishing I could recognize it. My programming was *all wrong*.

The mother—Jules—was certain I could be trained.

"Too old," Jonas said. "No one knows what to do with robots, and I've never in my life heard of one that could *learn* things it wasn't built to learn. It's not a person."

Sitting at their dining table in the corner of their warm little house, I folded my rust-red hands along its top. Two boys peeked over the kitchen counter. When Jonas powered me up the night before—to ensure I still functioned, too short a moment for me to learn their faces—I'd heard a boy coughing from the other room, his breathing rough as my own lungs full of rust and dust.

Without knowing who I was, I knew it sounded strange.

Emotions were sharpening, and I thought the two boys looked...nervous? Worried? The littler one chewed his smallest fingernail. Fear filled me, a strange sensation that pressed against the inside of my chest. I was drowning in my own breath. What would happen to me? I hadn't known them long, no more than minutes, really. But I knew nothing else.

I didn't want to go to another stranger.

Jonas cleaned me sometime before I woke, so I tried to work my old, rusted voicebox. "P-please don't sell me."

The father and mother stared. Only the boys looked unsurprised, smirking and exchanging glances while Jonas rubbed his scruffy cheeks. "What's that now?"

"I don't want to be—*sqlreeekk!*"

My voice broke in a harsh shriek, gears grinding. Pain registered somewhere in my wiring. Both boys stared with wide eyes and Jonas grimaced.

"Try not to speak too much, we don't know how much damage you have." His voice was gruff, irritated.

I wanted to hide, but had to ask again. "Please don't sell me."

Jules raised an unconvinced eyebrow.

"Let's keep 'im," the tallest boy interjected.

"Yes!" cheered the smaller. Jonas cast them a withering look, frustration winning over amusement. The older boy's voice was strange, scratched. He hadn't spoken much, and I was too shy to ask if last night's coughing had come from him.

"You don't wanna be sold?" Jonas asked.

"I don't wanna be sold."

The man had eyes like his boys, brown as dirt, that focused on me. "Why?"

For that, I had no answer. Why did it matter? I couldn't name a reason, only that the idea of leaving hurt. Like a bruise going deep to the bone.

I blinked at Jonas, lost for words.

He scratched his neck, muttering, "Dammit. Rotten lying scum of a salesman."

"Daddy, you're cussing again."

"Hush, Benny."

"Yes'sir," said the littlest boy.

"Jonas, maybe we should think on keeping him. He might be useful for something. We don't know," Jules said.

Gratitude flooded me, but I looked at my feet under the scrutiny of her gaze.

Jonas grunted.

She said, "No one around here would even buy him. He's junk in a place like this. Might as well try to get some use out of him."

She was disappointed. I knew it in the way she watched her husband, her eyes filled with his failure.

I wasn't the only one who saw.

"What am I supposed to do?" Jonas spat. "I can't run the farm on my own. Spend a little money on the damn robot, make more money in the field. Not a bad investment if I didn't get *screwed over*!"

I covered my ears, metal hands on metal head, hating the anger in his voice.

"Pop, you're scaring 'im," the eldest said.

Jonas sighed, rubbing his eyes. I knew his distress. Felt it deep in my iron chest. I wished to comfort them, all of them, but still didn't understand why I cared.

"He's a robot. Boys, go play outside." Jonas gestured at the door. He snapped his fingers, getting my attention. "You. Go with them."

My metal feet thumped on their wooden floors.

Jonas's voice faded as we left the house. "How are we supposed to pay it off if we can't even grow more crops? We're too damn poor. That bot was supposed to *help*, it's not my fault it's broken…"

We didn't speak, the silence fractured only when Jonas

stomped down the dirt road and Benny whispered to his brother, "Papa's gonna get in a fight, ain't 'e?"

"Shhh."

Fighting with the stranger who sold me? I wondered about that man. He must not even be half-decent to have done what he did.

He must have had less a heart than I.

We stood in the dirt near a horse barn, surrounded by corn-fields. I watched the leaves, the way they swayed and whispered. The sky, so strangely blue. We swayed like the cornstalks. Benny kicked dirt clods and his brother looked to be scheming.

"So, uh, you can talk?" Benny poked my metal shoulder.

"You are Benny," I told him, then turned to his brother. "You are...?"

"Simon. Do you know what you were made for?"

Made for? "No."

He coughed. "Did anyone name you?"

I blinked, tin eyelids clicking and clinking. It hadn't occurred to me. "No."

"Gotta name you," Benny declared. "I think he's a Thomas. He looks like a Thomas. Don't ya think?"

"Yeah." Simon seemed to taste the word. "Thomas."

Benny patted my back. He was a hand shorter than me, Simon just my height. "You're a Thomas."

"Thomas," I said.

. . .

"Thomas. Thomas?"

A hand taps my chest, fingers drumming a soft pattern, strange but not uncomfortable. Footsteps fade. Half-asleep with sunlight, the world is fuzzy and dreamlike.

Voices are arguing, the shop owners I serve and a new voice; warm and familiar. A man with a familiar voice holds a fistful of bills in one hand, leaning over the counter, back rigid. This man is large, more so than the shop owners, but he leaves when ordered. There is pain in the scrunch of his eyes and downturned mouth when he glances at me.

I should return to sleep. Or work and forget. But I remember the voices of the two boys, fresh and clear. With the owners in the back room, their voices irritated, I'm alone in the tractor shop, door opened by the man's rage.

A year has passed since I stepped outside.

I gaze at the lupine-blue sky, overwhelmed by an overload of color. A truck rumbles down the road, rusted red as my shell, disappearing around a bend in the road. Longing tugs me toward the tire tracks left behind. Fear hasn't appeared in so long, but it's been years since I've felt anything at all.

I step down the road, the sun warming my shell.

. . .

Benny and Simon taught me to play.

As sunlight wore on, I learned to catch a little red-stitched baseball. It spun past my fingers, colliding with my chest, a rumble like thunder covering the yard. My frame rattled.

"Thomas, are you okay?" Benny rushed me.

I knocked on my chest. The vibrations were odd. "I am fine."

"Really?" Simon asked.

"Yes, 'really.'"

The boys exchanged glances and shrugged.

Once reassured, they found my fumbles amusing. Laughter rang across the yard each time the ball ricocheted off me. Simon grinned, chuckling while Benny dissolved into giggle fits in the grass. The rattling amused me as well, or maybe it was their laughter.

"Hey Simon, that your new robot?"

I started, ball slipping to the ground. Three boys appeared from the cornstalks. Dirt covered their rough clothes just as Simon's and Benny's. The one in the middle, who'd spoken first, put me on edge.

Benny wrinkled his nose. Simon has a face like slate, cool and unreadable.

"He's *our* robot." Benny edged closer to his brother.

"What's he do?"

"Can he throw a ball?"

"We're teaching him to catch." There was calm in Simon's voice. It made me braver.

"What's wrong with him? He don't talk?"

Simon's hand covered Benny's mouth. The littler boy squirmed and scowled. A miniature version of his father.

"Don't your pa know when a robot's broken or not? My pa says he got *cheated*."

"Shut up, Dave," Simon warned, expression unbroken. Simon wasn't much older, but there was something old in his even eyes.

The other child—Dave—screwed up his face, his dirt-streaked cheeks puckering. Was he *jealous*? Despite my worthlessness, despite my age, I was rare. Something odd and unseen. It seemed right, and it amused me greatly.

My throat made a strange sound. Like Simon and Benny's laughter, but rusted and metallic. Unmistakable.

The trio stared. Simon's right eyebrow shot up. Benny giggled through his brother's fingers, and Dave's expression looked like Jonas's when he left to fight. The boy scowled and picked up one of the spare baseballs.

"Here, dumbass. Catch."

It ricocheted off my cheek, painless, but my body rattled and vision blurred. My hand shot out, the ball hitting my palm.

"Ugly robot!" Dave spat in my direction.

Simon's fingers curled. Dave hit the ground in a cloud of dust, his face pinched and shocked. Even Benny looked startled, and after a second, he whooped.

There was a pause like the silence before thunder.

The other boys tackled Simon. Benny shrieked and kicked, too small to do damage. "Get off him! Leave him alone!"

Dave pounced Simon, lips bleeding. "Your pa bought a junkbot! He's too stupid to know crap. He bought a junkbot!"

Simon coughed and spat in Dave's face.

I hated those boys, a strange emotion that burned and spun like gears in my chest. Wished I could stop them. I was useless for a mere moment.

I thought of the horrible noise when I spoke...

And ran at them, chanting until my voice broke. "You, you, you, you, you—*sqlreeekk*!"

The noise was vile as broken gears, loud and ear shattering. My throat seemed to crack. I never wanted to do it again.

But it *worked*.

Dave rocketed backwards, appalled, his friends scurrying away as if they couldn't move fast enough.

I charged them. "You, you, you, you, you—*sqlreeekk!*— you, you, you, you, you—*sqlreeekk!*—leave, leave, leave, leave, leave—*sqlreeekk—sqlreeekk!—SQLREEEKK!*"

I gave chase until they disappeared into the cornfield, plowing down the tall plants. The noise kept going. Stopping felt like trying not to breathe. My throat was raw. An old tractor full of rust and years. I didn't cough, didn't think I could, but I wished to sleep until my insides repaired. Was this how Simon felt?

Both boys wore uneven expressions. They sat in the dirt, clothes smudged. Dust settled around them. Benny stared; Simon's lips parted. His breath rattled, hitched, and choked. He slumped, breathing deep.

His eyes held the slightest awe.

Benny said, "Oh. My. God."

"You're staying." Simon's words, cracked like fall leaves, were a fact. There would be no argument. Benny nodded, earnest, crawling to his brother and hugging him.

Movement caught my eye. Jules was a statue on the porch. Arms crossed, hands kneading her shirt. Her eyes flickered between the three of us, expression unsettling but not angry.

She'd come to help but realized it wasn't needed.

I looked at the boys whispering on the ground. Simon seemed tiny, frail, so I gathered him in my metal arms. Back to Jules, with Benny trailing my heels.

I didn't find Simon heavy, but he was warm like the sun. And soft. So breakable. I was abrasive and solid beside him. Far from human. But he clung to me, arms woven about my neck. His heartbeat thumped against my sunbaked metal frame. It was fast but steady.

. . .

Jonas returned late. Simon and Benny cuddled within the same bed while I stood guard in the corner. I'd begged Jules not to shut me down, to let me stay and watch them. Protect them. Her eyes softened at the corners when she relented, the wax of a candle warming under flame. There was nothing to guard them from, but I was content.

Headlights swept the room, disturbing the shadows. Jules's footsteps padded along the hallway as the lights disappeared. The door creaked open and shut, the rhythm of soft voices whispering and mumbling. I didn't leave my corner until I heard a shallow, breathless noise like a hiss of pain.

My footsteps couldn't've been quiet, but neither turned when I peeked around the corner.

Darkness enveloped the house, their silhouettes haunting the kitchen. Jonas leaned against the sink, shoulders drooped, dripping exhaustion. Jules was beside him, holding his hands, running them under a stream of water. His fingers trembled, and they looked bloody in the night. He was speaking, but I couldn't make out the words.

I watched Jules, fascinated by the way she tended him, the softness in her movements. When she finished, she took his face in her hands. Kissed his lips, very lightly. He winced when he returned the kiss, tilting his head, his lip broken like his knuckles. Their movements were soft and otherworldly in darkness. Two moths circumnavigating one another. Foreheads rested together.

And I heard Jules whisper like a breath, "The robot stays."

. . .

I became useful.

It had nothing to do with farming. Jonas told me to stay with the boys wherever they went, and was gentler afterwards. My programming was correct.

Simon didn't improve. Benny couldn't explain his sickness, only to say that his lungs were filling with scars, it wasn't curable, and medicine could only do so much to help him stay a little longer. I couldn't help, but I could keep him safe.

I could carry him when he couldn't carry himself.

. . .

"I know what you're for," Benny told me once. We were hiding on the roof where a peach tree grew tall and wide, throwing itself across half the house. Fruit sagged the branches. Both boys swore it smelled of heaven. I copied Benny's posture under the branches, legs bent and elbows resting on my knees.

Simon lay on his stomach out of arm's reach, dozing in the sun. His breath rasped. I watched his eyelids—butterfly-wing thin, blue veins small as threads—and turned to Benny.

"You're here so that people will love you. And you love 'em. And the more you're loved, the more you're human. You're meant to do"—he gestured at us—"this. Which is good, 'cause Simon needs it. That's what Papa says. Works more magic than medicine. He's lived longer than they thought he would. And that's what you're for."

The idea was ludicrous. Ideas of a child. As little as I knew of robots, I knew love could not be programmed. But I felt no pulling desire or connection to my maker, whoever they were. There were only these people, this family. All I knew and all I wanted.

"Do you love us?"

"Can I?"

"I dunno. What do you think? Do you think you do?"

It was easy to say, so I thought it must be true. "I think I love you."

Benny nodded, satisfied. "Good."

When I looked over, Simon was watching. He smiled a little, and his eyes shimmered, reflecting something akin to joy.

. . .

Twice on the empty road—my legs stiff as ancient granite, neck bowed—I'm jolted from my reverie by the rumble of an engine. Each time, the pale blue SUV of the store owners appears in the distance. I hide once in the scratching leaves of a cotton field, once behind a thicket of blackberry bushes, and they never reappear.

I return my feet to the truck tracks, avoiding others I don't recognize, and pay no heed to the dirt filling my joints. The man who visited, he's important. That much I know. He'll lead me back to my boys. If I can remember how I lost them.

. . .

Benny was perched on my shoulders, a bird preparing for flight. Jonas eyed us protectively, unsure if he should intervene, but I held Benny steady and he let us be. Simon had that awed expression, brightened with the tiniest of smiles.

The neighbors were playing cornfield baseball. Benny cheered from my shoulder as Jules clapped beside me. Jonas drank a beer on the tailgate of his truck, his arm looped around his eldest son, quiet. Simon wriggled from his father's grip, trotting to the girl holding the baseball bat. Benny slid off my shoulders and I followed Simon, standing guard behind his shoulder.

The ball soared into the cornfield on Simon's second try, disturbing the tall stalks. I took Simon's hand when he walked around the bases, leading him back to the truck. Jonas picked his boy up and held him tight.

My hand was warm from Simon's fingers.

Benny appeared from the field, baseball retrieved, and placed the ball in Simon's hand while the older boy smiled.

I was watching Jonas weep.

. . .

Beside the cool of the creek, we hid from the autumn heat. Jonas was harvesting potatoes in a midday sun that made even the plants blister and curl. Benny walked barefoot in the creek while I followed along the shoreline, charging in the sunlight, afraid of rusting in the water. On the grassy bank, Jules sat with Simon in her arms, and Jonas joined us as the sun reached its peak.

Everyone was quiet, a fearful silence tightening my chest.

Simon watched us from his mother's lap, rolling the baseball between his fingers. Every time one of us met his eyes, he smiled, and something inside me cracked.

When Jonas joined us, he knelt to lay a hand on his son's forehead. He spoke with Jules for only a moment, then went inside and called the doctor.

. . .

My eyes closed, I didn't sleep but stood guard against something I couldn't fight. We were in Jules and Jonas's room. Their bed was big, their headboard redwood and carved with the letters J&J. It made me sadder.

The boys were cocooned between their parents. The doctor hadn't done much—Simon wasn't hurting, he'd assured us, and even Simon agreed. No pain touched his eyes. Nothing could be done but make him comfortable. He was best at home, everything safe and familiar.

He wore a mask the doctor said would help his breathing, but each breath rattled like a broken machine. I wished to give him my lungs, my body. Then I'd be useful. Like this, I was a waste. Every now and then Jonas's hand smoothed his son's hair, or Jules shifted closer. I didn't know if they were asleep or dozing.

I was ashamed. Simon was my brother, too, but I couldn't cry, not like Benny had when the doctor came. It weighed on me. A physical burden.

"Thomas?" Simon's voice was hardly there, a whisper of wind at night.

"Simon?" I matched his whisper. My voice was metal and grease, not as soft nor delicate, but no one stirred.

"Come 'ere."

It took me ages to walk the few steps in silence, but my joints didn't squeak. I crawled onto the bed near Jules's feet. The bed's softness was lost to me, I only knew the way it gave under my weight.

"Closer," Simon encouraged. I could see his little eyes now, heavy lidded and earnest. The mask was pale over his mouth, softening his words, a strange and foreign thing.

I did my best to crawl between Jonas's and Jules's legs until I touched Simon's feet. Satisfied with this, he settled. Benny shifted but didn't wake. I listened to my gears click and whir. I had lungs of some kind but didn't need to breathe. No noise came from my breath. The irony crushed me.

"Thomas?" Simon whispered.

"Yes?"

His words were slow and labored, deliberate. "I know you don't remember who you were before you came here. But I want you to remember. If you ever leave, remember all of us, okay?"

"I won't leave, Simon."

"Not while I'm here. I know. Just promise, please?"

"I promise."

"Promise me somethin' else?" he asked.

"Yes."

"Make sure Benny's okay. Protect him like you protected me. He needs your love too."

"I will."

He touched my iron hand. His fingers were far too cool. "Promise?"

"I promise."

"Thomas? I love you."

"I love you too, Simon."

I didn't move, not a bit. It was my place to guard them. I held Simon's hand until morning, when I could no longer hear his breathing, no longer feel his heartbeat.

. . .

It was days later that Jules led me outside, my wrist in her hand.

Her dress was gray. She didn't speak. Heat settled in the air, the sky a robin-egg blue. As if nothing was different and broken. The potato-field tractor sat abandoned. I couldn't find Jonas or Benny.

Jules took my chin, squeezed it in tight fingers and told me, "I'm sorry."

Benny came running when she loaded me into the back of the pickup, crying. I leaned down, too far to touch. Jonas scooped him out of reach. He rubbed my forehead with a rough hand. Looking into his eyes, I couldn't beg him to let me stay.

"It'll all be fine," he said like a lie.

Jules drove. Somewhere far where I would be bought for enough to cover the doctor's last visit, the money for Simon's medicine. Most importantly, I'd no longer be there to remind them of him.

I wouldn't be there to keep my second promise.

But I would remember.

. . .

My new owner shut me down. I stood in a corner amassing dust for immeasurable years, a relic, a collector's item. I woke in sunlight. Out of curiosity or ignorance, his cleaning lady had opened a nearby window and flipped my switch back on.

She looked scared and guilty when I stumbled out the back door.

. . .

Two men found me along the roadside, rusted from night-dew, head full of dust. They ignored my broken voice but cleaned my joints and set me to work scrubbing their tractors. I was always slow, trapped inside, never awake enough to think.

I couldn't farm, but somehow, I could help broken things.

Rust invaded my shell and eyes. I panicked when I forgot little things: The sounds of their voices, then colors of their eyes, their hair, their skin. The feel of the house, the little home amid miles and miles of cornfields. The heavy droop of the peach tree. Potatoes. A cool creek. Children in the baseball cornfield. I panicked when I forgot their names, their faces, and the promises I made.

I forgot what I was panicking about.

. . .

The sky weeps.

Rainclouds open, washing away the single thread leading me home. Hard-packed earth becomes a muddy river. Days and days the downpour lasts, flooding open fields, no trees to shelter me. I run until there is no trace in the mud and my joints stiffen with cold. All strength leaves with the sun, and my body bends, coming to rest in thick layers of mud.

Headlights cut the night, and I think the shop owners have come to drag me back. I want to shut down. A metal scarecrow, lonely and hunched in a roadside ditch. Dripping from another gathering of storm clouds. I blink against rain at the sound of a door opening, and a man stands before me, eyes wide and lips parted, a ghost in the night, until I remember him. Remember him like the cornfields and Simon's promise. Remember why his face brought me here.

"Benny..." My voice creaks, weakened with rust and water.

He makes a strange noise.

"Thomas, Thomas, Thomas." He slides down the ditch, slipping in the mud, his arms encasing me. "I knew it, I knew it was you. Oh Thomas, Thomas, Thomas."

"I'm sorry," I say, because I can't move my arms to hold him in return.

"Silly little robot." Benny's breath brushes my neck, deep and uneven. "I knew you'd never forget."

"Benny." I never want to lose that name again. The rain roars, headlights cutting the dark. Benny moves my frozen arms around his neck, whispering soothing nonsense.

He hauls me from the mud, enclosing us inside the dry warmth of the humming truck, and we're turning for home.

A LONELY SKY, A QUIET MOMENT

it is wintertime

and i am

curious:

why do robins stay

for blizzards

with red-breasted

arrogance

and blemishing

speckles

of young age

while geese flee

the snow,

their v the sharp

arrows of

elfland

piercing a

frigid sky

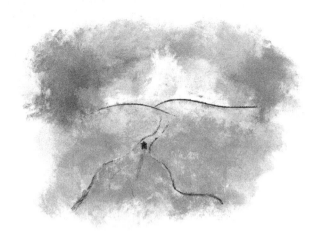

WE ARE NOT FAERYTALES

There are faeries in with the pigs. You holler at me until I'm stumbling out of bed, scraping my knee on a rough floorboard. I can hear you thumping downstairs, yelling louder than the pig when I bolt barefoot into the backyard.

The dawn is the color of scratched steel, the faeries spots of ashy skin crawling along the ground. The few with wings are gnawing at our pig's ears, at her tail. They twist themselves in my hair, latching onto my clothes and skin. We chase them out a hole in the netting the size of a small melon where they chewed their way in. You nudge the dead ones with your foot, your lips forming an ugly expression, and catch the piglets to check for wounds. The sow is bleeding from the faery bites, but it's nothing we haven't all endured. The chickens and goats in their own cages are hiding from the screeching, but their netting is untouched.

You turn away from me, your shoulders tight with anger or memories or something worse. I want to ask why you're even out of bed. What were you doing before you saw the little creatures slinking through the dawn? Then I see the satchel you've left on the porch, the scraps of cloth you're stitching together, and I remember you're leaving me.

I find a piece of shale rock big enough to cover the tear in the netting until I can patch the broken bits back together.

. . .

"Explain it to me again."

You haven't spoken all morning. Not since calling me out of bed. The bag you're making—the one to hold your things—sits beside you on the front porch like a wall between us. You've been nibbling one of the few carrots our garden produces, looking past the vegetable patch at something distant. Charting a course, perhaps.

"What don't you remember?" I ask, following your gaze. A dirt road leads down from our house into a forest of sorts. Much of the vegetation has been destroyed by faery teeth, but they never seem to have a taste for pine trees. Most of the forests left in the world are pine. What I wouldn't give for a pear tree. An orange. A plum.

"Where they came from," you say. "How they're dying out. How we're dying out. Who I was before I met you."

That last one stops me cold. I forget the bread I'm making and frown at the back of your head. At the scar hidden beneath your hair. The one that makes you fall asleep randomly—you already have this morning as you sulked on the porch—and any time you're still and thoughtful. The one that makes you forget the things you've lived or have been told a hundred times. Like why our world fell apart.

Or why you love me.

"They pulled themselves from somewhere out of the

ground," I say. "They didn't breed, they just…appeared. Everyone thought they'd be smart because they're faeries, but they're tiny things with tiny brains and they're dumb as hell. The stories everyone used to tell about them in books and around campfires are nothing but that: stories. They're dying because they ate everything in sight. Our crops, our livestock, sometimes us. Now they don't have any more food. They die almost immediately. And that's why we almost died out too."

You nod, but I don't think you remember. I'm never sure how much you remember of the things I help you relive.

"Your mother and mine were friends when they were chil- dren, but we never knew each other until after the faeries started showing up. I never got a chance to meet your family. They were gone when we met. You met my brother and my mother before…"

I don't need to finish for you to understand. As much as you don't remember, you know our reality. But you're silent, waiting for more, and it's something I can't give you. I can't tell you why you should love me, and especially not how.

So I say, "Only you know the answer to the last one."

You turn your chin side to side, not quite a shake of the head, not quite a nod, and I don't know what to make of it.

"Someone different," you say. "I was someone different, that's all I know."

. . .

There are clothes in your bag by evening, but you sleep on the lumpy mattress beside me. One foot hangs out from the covers, your arms curled beneath you like you're trying to keep every scrap of warmth inside your chest. Have you decided you'll leave? That running from me will hurt less?

I'm thinking on how your warmth is traveling through the blankets, how we haven't touched all day, when I hear wings and little feet. So small at first, like the edges of a dream, not quite real, but there nonetheless. I want to close my eyes against it, tell myself *no, no, it isn't real.* But then it's louder, a roar like sea waves, and I shake you, saying your name.

I hear you behind me as I throw a blanket around myself and race to the backyard. The vegetables will have to be safe under their netting, but the animals can be moved. They're meat, and the first things the faeries will hunt. It's been a year since so many of them appeared, but you remember what to do.

The swarm bites through my blanket, scratching my face. They're a dark cloud in the moonless night, like locusts or birds, a plague or a curse. I herd the pigs into the house, then the goats, while you guide the panicking chickens in the direction of our door. We lead them to the root cellar, because even glass windows have been broken by faeries.

My skin tingles and aches from little teeth and nails. You sit beside me in the dark, earth-smelling room. We have food down here, and water, but it shouldn't last long. Without food, they'll last only a few hours. I worry for our neighbors, but they're miles down the road, no way to reach them. Telephones haven't existed since I was a child.

You and I are still quiet, still wordless. But this time you drape your blanket across my shoulders, sharing your body heat, and I feel the weight and warmth of your arm pressed against mine.

. . .

There are several hundred of them, dead over our house and yard, when the sun rises. They never made it past our property. Perhaps we can find the ground they broke out of and cover it with stones. They're known to escape from the same hell holes as the ones that came before.

Their dead are too many to ignore. Already some of the first to die have begun to foul the grass with their rotting wings, leaving withered vegetation wherever they lie. Your lips have found that ugly expression again as you clear away the few that chewed into the vegetable patch. We gather them into crates before they decay further. Use a wagon and a wheelbarrow to haul them far down the road, where they won't taint the soil we use to grow our food.

When we stop long enough to rest under the shade of a bushy pine tree, I put my hand in your hair, tracing the scar with my fingers. You've told me different stories of how it happened. Attacked by faeries. Fallen from a cliff. An accident at a factory, back when they existed. I'd ask again, but I'd find myself with a different version of your life. Truth be told, I don't think you know.

Burning them causes terrible smoke, so we dig a hole large enough to hide them forever. Away from the forest, in a patch of empty land where nothing has thought to grow for a long time. On top, you toss the satchel you spent days making. I stare, my stomach knotting, and you shake your head.

"There are days I wake up and don't remember who you are," you say. "And that aches. And scares me. It's difficult to think of the whole world being like us, just hanging on, not willing to die out. And sometimes I think that walking down some unfamiliar road will make you and the rest of it less real, so I won't have to be afraid when I don't remember all the things that are important."

You take a breath like you're trying to fill your lungs with more air than they'll hold. "But leaving won't help. All it'll make me do is wake up and not have someone to remember for."

I close my eyes, leaning against your shoulder, opening them only when I feel your fingers on my arm, stroking where I was bitten and scratched. You kiss a cut along my collarbone, and help me bury the faeries, the drab pieces of cloth you stitched together.

Back home, we patch the torn netting, and there's only the rustling of the wind in the pines and the whisper of your breath. No faerytales, just us.

NEVER RISING

you sat on

iron cold stone

legs woven

beneath

you long

and short like

sea scrub

fingers flicking

pebble after

pebble into

a sulking surf

singing of tides

that once

languished

in valleys

swallowed

mountains whole

like sharp candies

tongues of waves

and fingers of salt

now never

rising never

rising never

rising

THE STARS AND THE RAIN

It rains the day my brother arrives. He steps onto Junian soil with a limp less prominent than the one I remember from childhood. And he stands there for a long moment, looking simultaneously lost and found. Getting soaked through.

The rain here is clear as anywhere, but likes to awaken the dormant algae growing invisible on every surface. The shuttle-pad is already shimmering purple when my baby brother gets his boots wet. I stand inside the shuttleport, watching Isaac slosh about like the ten-year-old he was when I left. He uses his cane to swirl the water while I try a little not to laugh, and mostly not to cry.

. . .

I jumped star systems when I was nineteen. Jun was exotic and licking its wounds from the recent ending of a war. When my girlfriends convinced me to go, I hugged little Isaac goodbye as he stood on shaky legs, smiling up at me. Waved to my parents and escaped my own personal war. My friends stayed a week.

I stayed much longer.

Armed with my camera and a splinter of high school journalism experience, I traveled every mile of the little planet I could. I talked face-to-face with Isaac almost every day on my tablet, then our parents would get on. They'd tell me what the doctors were saying. That he wouldn't last more than a few more months.

They kept saying this every couple of months.

When the largest news organization on Jun saw my collection of post-war photos and offered me a job, just me and my camera, I took it.

. . .

The first picture I took was in a bathroom stall. Someone had scratched words into the faux wood grains of the door. Some quote about love. I had to look it up—to find it was by a long-dead Earthling author—then sent the picture to Isaac.

I didn't ask my parents' permission before I took the job. But I asked my brother's.

. . .

We started communicating in this way. A picture sent across stars. Sometimes with a note scribbled electronically along the bottom. I printed his on precious, rare paper, so I could touch something he gave me. Tacked my wall with his pictures. Not the ones I took that won me awards.

We never discussed them when speaking face-to-face, those times when our parents would give the doctor's verdicts. I was steadily starting to believe the people who thought they knew the most really knew the least.

I was steadily starting to fear I never went home because I was afraid I'd see him die.

. . .

When he was fourteen, he sent me a photo of his doctor's framed MD.

Scribbled along the bottom: *When do you think they'll give up and just tell me they don't know anything? That I'll live as long as I damn well want to?*

I laughed so hard I couldn't see, then cried so hard I couldn't breathe.

. . .

At fifteen, he sent his perfect grades in school.

On the bottom: *I am the god of wisdom.*

. . .

When I was twenty-four, I sent a picture of my boyfriend, posed atop a mountain after a daylong hike.

What do you think?

. . .

His returning picture was of our parents together, cooking a familiar meal.

He's not good enough for you.

I rolled my eyes when I got it. Printed and tacked it on my wall.

A few months later, it turned out he was right.

. . .

When he was seventeen (I was twenty-five), I sent him three.

First: a ten-year-old boy from the most secluded village on the planet, dressed in blue-dyed papery pants, dripping with rain that puddled purple around his bare feet.

Bet you aren't this little anymore.

Second: a ghost town left by the war, with shattered stone buildings and roughened, decrepit wood houses.

Not our family. Not you and me.

Third: a sunset over Jun's sun-orange-tinted turquoise sea.

You need to be here.

. . .

When he was nineteen, a picture of our childhood house where he still lived. It was twilight, and hardly visible. My memories of that place weren't strong as they should've been.

If I said I wanted to come be with you, would you say yes? Why would you say yes?

. . .

Yes, come be with me. I wrote on what I sent in return. A copy of the oldest photo I had of him—when he was four years old.

Why? Because if this war-torn planet I've lived on these years can be so brave, then so can I. Because I thought I ran away the first time. Because I thought I was so afraid of watching you die I didn't watch you grow up. Because I miss you every day. And I'm still afraid, but I need you here. And I am so, so sorry.

Instead, I wrote a piece of that quote I first sent him off a trashy bathroom wall: *"Love is a growing up."*

. . .

Isaac sees me when I leave the shuttleport, getting my sandals wet with purple-algae-rainwater. We stand, awkward, grinning like idiots, him leaning on the cane that helps his twenty-year-old self walk, me with fingers wringing my shirt.

"I don't actually remember saying you could grow this much," I say, because he's tall. He is *so* tall. My head reaches his chest. Lanky too, like a cheetah pup growing into itself. He smiles and blushes. Swishes the water at his feet.

He says, "You're pretty as I remember."

I laugh, and hug him tightly as it rains, steadying him when he wobbles. "I'm sorry," I tell him, and feel some of the fear in me ease as he clings tighter, showing me the strength in his arms.

When he leans back, he's smiling brighter than I've ever seen.

I take up my camera and snap his picture in the rain.

AND SOMEDAY WE'LL SAY

let's abandon this ship,

break out treasures

from the crow's nest,

slap the lifeboat to water

faster than suns know

how to rise because

winter is coming

and we love this place

the way drought loves

the coming storm

OF WATER AND WOOD

When Easton is in the ground, you burn the unfinished wood. It's a stump, rough and unhewn—a soft brown like sparrow's feathers, with black streaks of leftover sap. Here and there, you think you might recognize the beginnings of a feature, a limb, or an expression.

Easton hated his creations unfinished.

You roll it to a bare patch behind your garden, sweating and puffing against the weight. It's wet with recent rain, slippery and hinting at decay. You douse it with kerosene, letting the flames rage, face burning in the orange glow.

By nightfall it's finished, a pile of ashes gray as the darkening sky. You take them in your hands, fistfuls at a time, and spread them over your husband's grave.

. . .

Deep in the night, the trees murmur. You slip from the bed to the window, touch the glass through the curtains. It's wet, cold, and smooth—a stone from the river. Darkness obscures even the shadows of the woods. Trees ring your house, your garden, the little section of earth you and Easton cleared for yourselves. Their branches intermingle, hug one another, pull and fumble in an unsteady dance. Birds' nests cling between branches like grasping fingers. Not Easton's birds, you don't think—the ones that sat on his shoulders, slept in his hands, and picked seeds from his offering fingers. Those birds, you haven't seen since last you saw him.

A weeping willow guards the grave. It seems so close to the ground, closer even to the house, its long branches brushing the dirt like fingers.

Cold from the floor, the window, and the unheated house sinks into your skin. You think about returning to bed, where carvings of foxes and forest creatures—more of Easton's hand-iwork—would guard you from the bedpost. But it's foreign without him, insubstantial and unsafe.

The bed quilt smells of him: wood varnish and soap. With the fabric flung around your shoulders, you feel weighed down and safe. You take it and sleep by the grave, curled within willow roots.

. . .

The preacher comes when you are chopping wood, his rusty wagon of a truck bouncing up the dirt road. The tree's hum is an uproar. Branches wail and collide, waves of leaves spiral-ing to the withered grass in a patchwork of fire. Black crows' feathers speckle them like ink. You would rake them up—leaves and plumage and all—but it's a losing battle against the woods. The preacher cranks his window down, one arm resting over the edge. His eyes trail the tangled branches behind you, but he waves nonetheless.

"Brooke." He smiles even as his eyes flicker to the grave hidden in the tree line. He'd spoken over the upturned earth when Easton was laid under, but the trees had been quiet things then.

You shove the last of the firewood under the eave, wiping your hands together. They're splintered and calloused, stiff and numb from work. It is strange to face another person, with your hair a mass of snarls, your face smudged and hands raw. But you feel safe, at least, in the clothes you wear. Easton's. Sweatpants bunched around your hips by the drawstring and a long-sleeved shirt that falls to your thighs and off your shoulder.

"Hello Father," you say. Hands buried in your pockets, you walk to his truck. The old man's storm-cloud-blue eyes are soft and concerned, crinkled at the edges. When you were younger, his hair was straw colored. It's paper now, rough and thick with a texture like grass. The calm in his demeanor is soothing, but he doesn't leave the safety of his truck.

"Whole forest's like this," he says, pointing to two trees whose trunks have collided with a sound like buckshot. You put your hands on the truck's window ledge, let the iron-cold seep into your fingers, and watch the birds scattering from the woods with something akin to longing. "There's hardly no wind. Just ruckus. It's downright eerie."

"Old woods get odd like that," you say, then wince. Easton said such things, but he loved his trees. And he was good at his magic. It wasn't something you understood—still can't understand. The townsfolk used to think him odd. They were wary of his ways until he was kind to every one of them. Still, suspicion was a hard habit to break.

"Big ol' oak came down on Mrs. Mavis's barn last night. Nothing got hurt. Scared the daylights out of some chickens though." He chuckles. "Radio says big storm's rolling in. I'm headed to town for groceries. Don't suppose I can pick up anything for you?"

You glance at the house, untouched by the forest's fallen branches, with all its stacked firewood. In the cabinets, there's enough canned food for a week. More in the fridge. You can smell the storm in the breeze, electric and stirring. It fills your lungs, clears your head. The trees, in their frenzied mourning, put you on edge more than any approaching thunder. How they can grieve so loudly, for the neighbors and the wolves and the birds to hear, is beyond you. Maybe your body wasn't born for that kind of grief. You feel soft and heavy, as if you slept it would last ages.

"I'm fine," you say. "Have everything I need."

He nods, touching your hand with crepe paper fingers before giving the woods a last squint and driving away.

. . .

At night, you dream you're under the earth beside Easton. Soil constricts on all sides. You taste it in your mouth, under your tongue, sharp and mossy, full of earthworms. The pointed ends of feathers and bird bones twist your hair. Your toes and fingers become roots, sinking farther down, anchoring you to willow roots. Your skin is buried leaves. Your lips sprout flowers, pushing through the topsoil. Easton is all bark and tree roots. They wrap around your ribs. Through the cavern of your heart.

. . .

When you wake, an old maple has thrown itself across your garden. The storm is here, rain lashing the window. Even inside it smells of water. Water. Mud. Damp wood.

For a moment, you think you see something pulling itself free from the shadows of gnarled roots. But you wipe the tears from your eyes and can't find it again.

No matter how many quilts you pull over your head, you can't recreate the feeling of all that earth.

. . .

Under the sun, the storm breaks for a few hours. Clouds hang in the distance, ominous and heavy with water. The power went out sometime in the night. You build the fire warm and crackling, hang the laundry outside to dry. Walk around the fallen maple, around the grave. The creek hedging the trees is clogged, swollen with water and fallen leaves. The trees sway, a chorus of restless noise. Wind snatches at your hair, twining it around your neck, down the back of your coat. Your husband's hands are in the wind, around your fingers, against your waist, holding you tight. A kiss against the neck. The lips.

But that's not quite true. Easton was something other than this. He was alive. Warm.

The sheets snap on the clothesline, coiling and tugging at their restraints. Great, white beasts. When the clouds hang lower, the storm returning, you gather them from the line. Clothes first. Socks next.

Sheets last, and there is a shadow behind them that was not there before.

It doesn't flicker with the wind, doesn't move within the fabric. No figment of your imagination. You think of the fallen maple, lying in your garden like a beached whale. Whatever nightmare your half-dreaming eyes dreamt were tangled in the roots. You touch the sheet, twirling it around your wrist. The shadow moves, wraps round itself, and you clutch the sheet to your chest.

Child's eyes blink at you.

Green, brightly so, like fresh leaf buds. Too large for the thin face, lips out of proportion. With its tiny body and willowy limbs, it could be a child. But it's like nothing you've ever seen. Its body—all naked, neither male nor female for all you can tell—is river-stone gray and smooth, flecked with bits of black and silver. A robin's egg and just as frail. Ribs and bones are there, just underneath, jutting out everywhere. Thin and shivering.

"Who…?" you breathe, trying to raise your voice over the wind. It's odd from disuse. "What *are* you?"

Those words sound cruel coming from your lips. The little thing is trembling, hands fisting in front of its stomach, trying to cover its nakedness. Feathers outline its skin, and you think of Easton's birds watching from the wild branches or shedding their down to make parts of this creature. The child shakes its head, licks its lips, as if it can't figure the words trying to break free.

It whispers with a voice as tumbling and unsteady as water, "Eas-Easton."

A hollow ache begins behind your breastbone. Your hand covers your mouth. Something like anger burns your throat. Shame should stopper the venom in your words, but it spills forth nonetheless. "You're not Easton. You're just the woods. Go back."

It whines, a slow, animal whimper of pain that chills your

bones. "I c-can't."

You step back, hugging the sheet. This is what the forest offers. It grieves your husband with noise and crashing trees. And it leaves some half-living thing for you. Quivering amongst your sheets.

"Go. You're not Easton's and you're not mine. Go *back*."

You hide in the house, for hiding is all it can be called— cowering against the door, face pressed into the sheet. The house is warm, leftovers of love in the walls. What would Easton think of you now, leaving a child for a storm to drive away? Even the little forest thing it is. Back to the cold, loud woods. Alone. You wonder what the neighbors will say, the others in the town. What rumors will haunt your home. You only think on them a moment.

You take the big quilt from the bed. Hold it tight around your shoulders. Already, the smell of him is beginning to fade.

When you return, the child is hunched. Crying. Its tears don't slip the way they would on human cheeks. They catch on dry stone, leaving dark trails. You touch its hair, all ropey and thick, more like the smallest roots of grass than the fine stuff around your shoulders. Its skin is cold but thrumming with life. Some type of forest magic.

It looks up at you while it weeps. "I'm l-lonely."

"I know. So am I."

You nest it in the quilt. Pull it against your chest. Its hands tighten in your hair, body light as dry wood in your arms. The rains return. Kneeling by the fire, you hum a lullaby you can't remember the words or story to.

You think you hear bird-song outside, chattering like the woods. The child no longer cries, curling against you, whispering words like the murmur of leaves. You smile, and hide the sweetness in the child's hair. Kiss its stony neck. Sing until the trees outside calm, and you feel its heartbeat against your chest. Alive and warm.

FATE

I heard in the dying breath of flowers
whisperings of threads woven by graces
the beauty of one did not
outweigh the wisdom of
witnessing transient time

I am a selfish wretch
I would kiss the
withered foot of
the ancient crone to
dance with your flesh
through the dappled
weavings of time

FROZEN MEADOW, SHINING SUN

My sister has been missing three days when the fox appears.

My ona returns with his small group of men, my sister not among them. They walk exhausted and slumped, long beards catching heavy snowflakes. They shiver under their bearskins, and his eyes are dark and empty, crying of loss. A day and a half of searching through a gathering storm, and he still can't find his eldest daughter. My totto, my mother, wails, and her own sister, belly swollen with a coming child, gathers her close.

The snow swallowed my sister, Ona says. She lost herself in the storm.

I try to imagine it. My sister losing her way. Such things don't happen to Aimi. Her feet are sure of their path; her eyes find their way where others would not. She knows the woods, the same ones I fear; the snow couldn't have changed such knowledge.

The eyes of the other villagers follow my ona, then rest on me where I stand half-hidden behind our family's hut. Some of the young men are still nursing wounded pride from my sister denying them all her hand in marriage. A few of them frown at me, and their parents shoo them away. The adults are not angry, but they stare. They've known me my entire life, and for that reason, some are curious, suspicious. They think a girl will always know where her sister hides. But I don't know. I *should* know.

The wind is ice-cold, bearing snowflakes from far away. I catch a scent in it, a smell I fail to name or truly recognize. It makes me think of my Aimi. It's sharp and bitter and warm at once, and it's gone before I can blink. When I turn towards the woods, I almost think I've imagined it. As I slide a toe across the border of the tree line, my stomach flutters like spirits are dancing in it, pounding their feet. Ask after what I fear, and I can't tell you. There's no sense to it, nothing I can control, nothing I can soothe. No fearlessness in my soul.

I touch the trunk of the closest tree. The storm is swirling, regaining its vigor. Tendrils of cold slip through my bearskin, and my feet sense the coming ache of standing in the snow too long.

"Aimi?" I whisper.

The wind calls, but no one else. The tree trunk shimmers a coating of ice in the cold light of the winter-white sun. Where has my sister gone? Why would she leave me the way she did?

I beat the trunk with a snow-rotten stick. Shivers of ice fly in my face, stick to my hair. And there, screaming at a tree that refuses to speak, a flash of red catches my eye.

The fox is staring, blinking ice-white eyes rimmed with black. Its ears and paws are tipped with fur so dark it seems like bits and pieces of it are disappearing into the shadows of the woods. Thin and waifish; the snow drifts seem to swallow it up. The red that caught my eye amongst all the white is its foot, limp and blood-crusted, from a fight with another animal or a wayward arrow from one of the hunting parties; it's difficult to tell.

Nine separate tails drape the snow behind it.

I sink into the snow, fingers aching with the cold.

"Kitsune," I breathe. A fox spirit. I reach out a hand.

My sister has always reminded me of a fox, for the way the woods embrace her, for the long shape of her face and the quickness of her eyes. For the *strangeness* of her eyes. One all blue like the darkest river water; the other black as if someone sprinkled flecks of obsidian into it, so unusual for our people. Not a trace of my parents resides in her features; none of me. She is ours but doesn't look it. She could be a kitsune, although she laughed the once I asked.

"Aimi?"

It growls, showing ivory teeth. When it backs out of the snowdrift, I can see that it is male, and my hand drops. If it isn't Aimi, it could be dangerous. Benevolent spirit or demon, there's no way for me to tell.

The full of the storm is upon us, numbing my ears and ripping at my dark hair. The air is crisp, smelling only of the blizzard. I cast a glance towards the village. Our cluster of thatched homes will be buried by the time the moon rises. My ona will be in the home of the village head, discussing my sister and the village's need to hunt game through the snows. My totto will be with her sister through the night, expecting the child to come. I will be alone in the house with a fox spirit outside, and that frightens me.

I run home, but the kitsune doesn't follow; simply watches with too-bright eyes. I stoke the fire pit near the front of the hut, crack the door to watch for movement, and, when there is none, crawl within the hanging mats of Aimi's bed.

After a time, I sleep.

. . .

When I was young, not yet past eight years, my sister took me far into the woods. My memories of that time are a child's memories, still ethereal and strange but real as any other. I accepted the strangeness then the way one accepts the sunrise or the rain.

It was early spring, some stubborn bits of snow still refusing to melt. The mountains in the distance seemed frozen and fresh. Many of the men had prayed for a good catch and safe hunt to Kim-un Kamuy, god of bears and mountains, and left in search of deer and bears still sleepy from hibernation. Our totto was cleaning early caught salmon, preparing the meat to be boiled and dried. Aimi was always watching, waiting for opportunities, and when our totto's back was turned, she fled with me into the new growth of the forest.

I enjoyed it for a while. The spirits within the trees frightened me when my sister wasn't by my side, but with Aimi I was free to explore. I couldn't explain the safety she brought; all I knew was the freedom of it. My sister always knew where the forest treasures were. A tree that leaked honey, or berries that bloomed early. Maybe we would catch salamanders by the smaller fork of the river. But Aimi ran on, face set with determination. I'd never seen her that way, and it kept me silent as I struggled to keep pace with her longer legs. She refused to release my hand.

We went farther out than allowed, and I was hopelessly lost. Finally frightened enough, I began to whine.

"Hush," she told me, expression brightening, "I want to show you something."

The woods broke very suddenly with her words, and a meadow stretched out before us. I turned back, blinking in the sunlight, and the outline of the mountains burst against the horizon. I was too young to realize that they should have been before us instead of behind us and were too far away for our little legs to have crossed.

An old fox greeted us at the edge, three-tailed and red like fire. I was so small that her snout reached my neck, smelling of the cloying musk of foxes, thick and odd, like dirty metal gripped in my hand. She came to Aimi like one of the village dogs, completely unafraid, and kissed her cheek.

There were others in the clearing. A gathering of many different colors. The clouds were drizzling, a warm, springtime rain, the sun shining through. I could taste the smell of rain and wet grass on my tongue. And something different, bitter and sweet all at once. I knew the stories, the fate of those uninvited to kitsune weddings, and I tugged on Aimi's arm, fearing a fox's teeth in my throat.

"It's fine. I'm invited," she said, releasing my hand. "Trust me."

I plopped down among the grasses, a nervous ball of little limbs, watching my sister mill about the fox spirits. The bride and groom were gorgeous in their human form, their features much sharper than my sister's. They were naked in the clearing once they lost their fur, but I knew we were far enough away from home that no one would to find us. Not all the kitsune changed, but those that did gave me soft, curious looks and did not pay me any mind.

Once wed, the couple retreated to a hut in the border of the clearing, its walls woven so tightly with bamboo that I didn't notice it until they disappeared into its shadows. I wanted to follow, to see what magic had created it, but couldn't gather my courage.

My sister took me home late that evening, humming to herself. She swung our hands between us, and I felt a part of something that was too strong and bright to ever break.

"Don't ever tell anyone," she said, bumping me with her hip.

"I promise."

I kept my promise, but curled now within my sister's bed, I remember a kitsune pup my sister had spoken to those years ago, white-furred with bits of black on his ears and paws.

. . .

I wake to the howling of the storm outside, the wet pad of snowflakes against the hut, and a distinctively animal whine at the door. I loosen the shutters of a window, peeking over the edge. The fox is balled against the door, shivering under the blinding snow. Pity closes my throat, dampening my fear. When I unlatch the door, he looks at me warily, head low, eyes raised, unsure if I'm to be trusted. I open it further, feeling the heat from the hut rushing out and the smell of something odd and magical rushing in. I am overwhelmed with the expectation that my sister will be standing here, instead of this furry little creature. It passes quickly but seems to lodge a sliver of itself in my heart.

"Come in," I say.

He hesitates then scampers past, standing opposite the fire, peering around, ears perked. His tails twist within one another as he wags them nervously. It's the oddest sight, beautiful and

SHORT STORIES & POETRY

unreal. I sit and offer a strip of bear meat balanced in my palm. He sniffs, dips his head and takes a step, limping on his injured back leg. His eyes stay on my face, unnervingly wise, before taking the treat delicately from my hand and flopping down at my feet.

I maneuver my way to his back foot, but he doesn't mind when I brush his tails aside. How he is so tame, even being a spirit, is beyond me. When I lay my hand on his leg, above the wound, his eyes flicker back and stay on me, but he rests his head on his paws. I dress the small wound with honey to keep out infection and bandage it with strips of cured salmon skins.

With nothing to do, I sit and drink in the sight of a spirit warming himself by my fire. His musky dirt scent, strangely attractive, fills the hut.

I want to fetch Ona from the meeting house, but I don't know if he'll approve of a kitsune in our home, especially after Aimi's disappearance. He might take it as a bad omen. Totto was always more tolerant when Aimi and I brought back injured creatures, but even she might be suspicious. And I wouldn't know how to get her from her sister's house without spilling the secret. Others would kill the spirit in a heartbeat, both to drive away demons and for the meat.

The fox is watching me over his shoulder, eyes sharp, as if he senses my thoughts. I wish he would change to a form I can speak to, but I doubt he remembers me from all those years ago.

On the other hand, why else would he come to *me*?

"Aimi?" I ask again, "Do you know Aimi, my sapo, my sister, did she send you?"

He blinks and whimpers, head on his paws, unhelpful. The door to the hut works open, my totto's feet against the threshold, and the fox is gone before I can speak, disappearing within the curtains of Aimi's bed. I am stunned, hands half held out, mouth open. Door shut, Totto stares at me, something hard in her dark eyes. I feel like a chastised child, although I've done nothing but allow a mild-mannered spirit into our home.

"Opere…" she says, her voice cracking under a strain I don't understand. "Where is it?"

"Totto…?" I ask, certain she couldn't have seen the spirit in the storm, not from her sister's hut.

"Huci-Resunotek saw you take a kitsune into this home. Where is it?"

I lower my eyes. The old grandmother sees everything. I should have known. But how she told my totto so quickly is beyond me. "Totto, he's kind and tame."

"How do you know anything about such matters?"

Her tone lets me know it isn't a question, and I bite my tongue, thinking of the sunshower wedding Aimi led me to all those years ago. All I know is they never sought revenge on us. Suddenly, I think I must check the clearing of the wedding, even in the winter. The bamboo hut. Where else would Aimi run when upset? But I doubt I could find it on my own. I doubt I can step in the woods on my own.

Totto is checking the individual bed curtains, ripping at them with a vengeance. She finds the little fox and snatches at his tails, dragging him out, his nails making hard scratches in the dirt-packed floor.

She grabs his muzzle with her other hand, stronger than I would have imagined her soft round body to be, and snarls, "What have you done with my Aimi, fiend?"

"Totto! Totto, he's hurt!" I grab her arm, but she shrugs me off, and I land backwards trying to help. The kitsune does not bite or scratch but spits a necklace at my totto's feet, a long chord with a glass ball on the end, dragged from Aimi's things. My totto's hand slips from his tails, her shoulders hunching as she stares at the piece of jewelry. The kitsune whines and nudges it with his nose, backing towards the door pointedly.

My heart flutters, a mixture of excitement and fear. "He knows where Aimi is."

My totto shakes her head, gathering the necklace into her fingers. "I should have known. She's all me."

I get to my feet, touching her shoulder. I've never seen her like this, cruel to a living thing. In my fifteen years, I've never seen her so sad.

"Totto?" I whisper, frightened to ask for an explanation.

She takes my hands and hugs me. Her embrace is all-encompassing, and I feel the strength in her arms needed to wrestle that fox from the bed. She smells warm and comforting, like fire smoke, and I lean back, wondering at her.

"You're all of your ona, do you know that?" she asks, more to herself than to me. "Aimi is all me. I can't believe I let this happen."

I see the kitsune over her shoulder, his eyes low-lidded, knowing. He understands her words, even when I don't. I think of Aimi and her fox face, the way she loves the woods. The way my totto never slides a foot past the border of the trees but always gazed longingly after us when we ran in. I thought I got my fear of the forest from her, but she wasn't afraid at all.

Aimi is all me.

"Totto," I ask, knowing how horrible this will sound if I'm wrong, "are you...like him?"

Her breath is more of a shudder, and I know I've stumbled across her secret. I hug her tighter, trying to imagine it. It's difficult to believe, but she's always been magical in my eyes, for no reason I can explain. She doesn't *look* like a kitsune, like the others I saw in the meadow that day, but perhaps all her years as a human have dulled the wildness in her. The softness of her has hidden all the sharp angles and features. Maybe she has given it all to Aimi.

"Does Ona know?" I ask.

She sighs, and her voice cracks as she speaks, "I think he suspects, but he won't give voice to it. Opere, he must *never* know. You must never tell him. If you tell him, I must leave."

I feel cold in the warmth of the hut, at the thought of my totto leaving. But there's something I know for certain, "You should tell him. He loves you too much to make you leave."

She sounds exhausted, "Opere..."

"Tell him. I'm going to find Aimi." I say, pulling away. My totto's eyes are red-rimmed with worry and hurt, but I smile. "We'll be back."

"No, I will go. I still know the woods better than you."

The kitsune barks, shakes his head. Points his snout towards me, as if only I am allowed. As if Aimi only asked for me. Somewhere inside my soul, I feel warm.

Totto turns to the fox at the door. The creature has averted his eyes, having the decency to be timid. No other animal would think to do such a thing.

"Take your form." Totto says, her voice no longer quite so harsh.

The kitsune blinks, but his bones pop, pure fur retreating into his skin until there is a tall, startlingly naked young man crouching by the door. His eyes are the oddest color blue, his skin pale, hair black as his ears had been, face lovely. His expression is sad, eyes shimmering in the firelight.

"You had better keep her safe," my totto says, and I don't know whether she's speaking of me or Aimi.

He nods, a strange movement, more used to being an animal than a man. His voice is lilted and gorgeous. "I love her."

"I know," my totto says, eyes softening. "Now get out."

I stare as he shifts back into the shape he's most comfortable with, watching me expectantly. My sister is in love with a kitsune. I'm not surprised, although I feel as if I should be.

I wrap myself in my bearskin and another for Aimi, kissing my totto's cheek.

"We'll come home," I swear again. "Promise to tell Ona."

"Be careful. Be safe," she says, and doesn't promise.

I shut the door behind me. The kitsune is sitting at the wood's edge, and I crunch through the snow towards him, stopping beside the trunk of a tree.

"She's loved you for a long time, hasn't she?"

He whines and bobs his head. His thick fur whips every different way in the storm's wind.

"I don't know why she left. Why now, of all times?"

He knows what I'm saying, every word of it, but his eyes only shimmer and blink. I think I'll know the answer soon enough.

He limps away, and I stop. It occurs to me finally that I will be hunting for Aimi in the woods, at night, in a storm, without her there. I've never been in the woods without my sister. Maybe this is what I was afraid of all long—that my sister would disappear into the trees and never come back. At least when I was in the woods with her, I knew that wherever she went I would not be left behind.

Be brave. I tell myself. *I'm in the company of a kitsune. I'm strong enough for this.*

The spirits in the wood are kind, if they show their faces at all through the harsh snow. I breathe, try to find the shape of the mountains through the snow, and when that fails, follow the spirit blindly into the storm.

. . .

I think of Aimi to keep my thoughts even, unafraid. I try to understand.

At seventeen, she is past old enough to have taken a husband, yet she refused every young man who tried for her heart. She never gave reasons, not even something as simple as disliking the boy.

Three days ago, our ona was trying to reason with her for an explanation, and his gentle prodding upset her. I remember her crying and rising to leave. She asked me to walk with her, but I only tried to coax her into staying. The hurt in her eyes then won't leave me now.

With the kitsune leading me through the snow, I understand what she was frightened to tell us, but why she suddenly thought she had to leave, I can't imagine. Maybe if I'd just walked with her, she'd have told me, and she'd be safe with us at home.

Maybe if I'd walked with her, she would have trusted me with her secret.

. . .

I remember the trek to the kitsune meadow taking hours in the warm easy travel of springtime, but it seems such a short time now. I keep my head down against the cold, watching the limping paw prints before me as a guide. Every few minutes, the kitsune turns his head to check on me. I wish I could read the emotions in his eyes.

I am shivering even under the extra bearskin I brought for Aimi, but soon the woods spread open before us. The meadow is unfamiliar with so much snow, but the storm has eased, leaving a silence so deep it makes noise of its own. Snow cracks. A shining cold sun peeks over the trees, shimmering against the crystals of snow, but another storm is brooding on the horizon, embracing the mountains. If anything, it looks to be worse than the last. I wonder how many days it will rage and if Aimi and I will return home before it falls.

The hut looks the same as in my memories, green in the whiteness, smoke drifting from the hole in its snow-covered roof. It hasn't lost any of the mystery it possessed in my childhood. I'm ashamed it took me so long to realize that this is the first place my sister would run.

The kitsune trots across the frozen meadow, quicker than before, leaving me to stumble along behind. He pauses before the hut, feet planted in the snow, expectant. I lay my hand on the wooden door, almost touching my head to it, breathing in as deeply as I can. The cold air stabs my lungs, but the scent of the hut is strange and familiar at once. Bitter and warm, like the earlier ache that settled in my chest.

It feels *right* somehow, but I'm suddenly nervous. What will my sister say? I can't imagine returning home without her.

The kitsune glances between me and the door, nudging my knee with his head. When I crack it open, he slides inside.

My sister's voice drifts out. "Did you find her?"

"Aimi?" I ask, forgetting my nerves and pushing away the door.

It's darker in the hut than I would have imagined, the warmth of the fire tingling my cheeks. Nothing so magical or mysterious that I can see, besides the bamboo forest woven into the walls. And the aroma of a home that crashes over me, much stronger than anything the wind carried my way. There are reed mats stretched across the floor, dry and crackling under my feet. I can make out the silhouette of a bed stretched along one wall and the form of my sister sitting curled by the fire.

Her voice is scratchy, hardly a croak. "Opere...?"

My heart pounds with relief, my throat wanting to cry, and I shut the door to hurry to her side. The fire gives off some heat, but still I cuddle beside her and wrap her in the bearskin to share warmth. If only to be closer. Her breath is cool on my face, and her one blue eye shimmers in the darkness, brighter than the other. The tattoos around her lips, marking her womanhood, seem nothing more than a shadow in the lack of light. She laces an arm around me, head on my shoulder.

The only noise beside the cracking fire is the kitsune's panting, his breath hot and dog-like. He lays with his chin on her leg, watching her face with tender eyes. Orange firelight leaps and dances over his coat, casting strange shadows.

We are quiet for countless minutes, holding each other close. Eventually, when the new blizzard has begun to howl around the hut's walls, she speaks. "You followed him here? Through that storm?"

"Yes."

"You went into the woods without me."

I'm embarrassed, and a little proud. "Of course, I worried for you. I missed you."

Her hands grip my shoulders tighter. "I'm so sorry."

"No need." I say, shaking my head, then smile against her neck, feeling like teasing her, giddy with relief. "You're in love."

"We are one," she says, and her voice cracks at my intake of breath. "Months ago. I wanted you to be there for the wedding, but I was afraid..."

Maybe I should feel betrayed, for her secrecy, for marrying a creature so unusual and wild, but I feel something warm fill me, knowing how happy she must be with him. I snuggle closer, letting her know she's forgiven. "That's silly, to be scared."

"I know," she mumbles, but still, there is relief in her voice.

"I'm sorry too, Aimi. For not coming with you when you asked. I knew you wanted to talk to me, but I didn't come—"

She touches my cheek, sighing contently. "It's all right, as long as you're here now."

We're still for a few moments more, before I ask, "Why did you leave all of a sudden? Aimi, I don't understand—"

"I didn't want to," she says, stopping me, stroking her husband's ear. He whines and licks her hand. "I wanted to stay home, I did. But I didn't know how...I didn't know how to tell you..."

She works my hand under her garments, pressing against the warm skin of her belly. It feels soft and flat, no different than any other day, but the gesture speaks for itself.

"Oh!" I gasp, an inexplicable amount of joy filling me. "No wonder you're moody."

"Opere!" She's trying to sound affronted, but there's too much surprise in her voice. I giggle, and the kitsune yips. If a fox could laugh, this is what it would sound like. My giggle turns into a full laugh. Aimi pinches me, her lips forming a shaky smile. I squeeze her neck and wrestle with her gently. She rests her cheek against my shoulder and doesn't speak again.

The kitsune's eyes are closed, his head lying on my sister's leg, face pressed into her stomach. I think of home. "Aimi, Totto is a kitsune too."

She lets out a harsh breath, touching her chest in surprise.

"We want you home. We're going to make Ona understand."

There is silence in the little bamboo hut, until I feel hot tears on my neck that are not mine.

"You know we love you," I say.

"I know," she whispers, "but the village…"

I grimace, knowing the rest of the place we call home will not take so kindly to a kitsune and their child, even if they are bonded through marriage. But our totto did it, and I won't let my sister run away forever, even if only our little family will know the truth.

"Can you be brave, for me?" I ask.

"I don't think it's that simple."

"It's the best way to start, isn't it?"

She takes a breath. "I…I'm not going back to the village, Opere."

All the air leaves my lungs, and I pull away enough to see her face. It's streaked with tears, but her eyes have that same, strange determination. I refuse to believe it. "Aimi, we can find a way—"

She shakes her head. "I don't think Totto is going to tell Ona."

"She will," I say with absoluteness.

Aimi looks at me out of the corners of her eyes. "Did she really say that?"

I open my mouth, but no sound answers. I remember the expression our Totto wore when I asked her to promise. How *she didn't promise*.

Aimi reads the answer in my eyes, and the smile she gives me holds no happiness. "Secrets like this can't keep themselves."

"But Totto—"

"Totto is just *one* kitsune, and she gained the trust of everyone around her. She never went into the woods, and that's giving up what she was. I can't bear that. And neither can he." She spreads her fingers in her husband's coat.

Fox eyes blink at me, and I look down at him. His face, even so much like a dog's, is sad, apologetic. He's hurting for his wife, for the new sister he's only just now begun to know. He licks my hand, and the realization of why I'm here crashes over me like a spring waterfall, isolating and cold. Pressing down on my shoulders, making it difficult to breathe.

I finally understand what she means. There's no home left for her in our little village.

I am here to say *goodbye*.

And if I do, I may never see her again.

I raise my head to find her gazing into my eyes, begging me to understand. When I don't speak, she cries. Aloud, this time; not silent, gentle tears. Covering her face with her hand. Fear makes a raw wound inside me. More acute and deep than any unease the woods inspire; immediate as a broken limb.

Her hands in mine, I lean my forehead against hers, eyes closed. There are new things I refuse to believe in. That all the years our parents have been together, that all the love they've shared and given to us, can be shattered by something so small as our totto's other skin. That this is the end of our family.

That I will let my sister walk away, into these woods, without me.

"What if I stay?" I whisper.

Aimi sniffles, eyes flickering to mine. "What?"

I hold her gaze long enough to know the words I say are right and true and I can't simply walk away from what is here in this little hut. That it is something strong, bright, and unbreakable. "I'm not letting you run away. I'm *not*. Even if you never come back, what if I stay?"

Awe has written itself across my sister's face, and it's a time before she finds words. "You can't just run away too—"

Her husband whines, rolling to his feet. I wince as I hear his bones popping, but he doesn't appear to be in pain as he wraps a blanket around his now-human self. His eyes have many of the same emotions as my sister's, and he leans against her to whisper in her ear. They share a long look I don't understand.

"My cousin," he says, tripping over the words in a tongue he's not used to. "She is not far outside. If you'd like to stay out the storm here, she can carry a message. To your mother. So she understands."

We both look to Aimi, him calm and expecting, me fearful that she won't want me here. She never takes her eyes from me, weighing her thoughts with everything she knows.

"You're going to have your own life very soon, and I won't let you give that up to stay with me. But until then—" She touches my cheek softly. "I'd love to have my sister here."

I watch a small but genuine smile curl her cheeks, and I wrap my arms around her neck.

She turns to the bright expression on her husband's face. "Will your cousin go now?"

"Yes. I'll tell her."

He leans over to kiss her in a way that's familiar. Tender and sweet, not too far from the kisses my ona gives my totto.

When he's in his fox skin once more, he slips out the front door, into the howling snowflake-laden wind. Aimi and I watch him go without speaking, without needing to. Contentment has settled over me, tinged with sadness for our parents and the hardship that may follow once this storm has blown itself out. Wherever she goes, I'll be right there for her and the little child she carries, until I'm ready to begin my own life.

I take her hand and hold it tight, listening to the snow and the howl of a fox outside, breathing in the smell of home.

GOBLIN MARKET

Come sell me your wares

Come sell me your fears

A kiss from a frog

And mermaids' tears

This goblin market spreads

Across dragon-hide scales

For the tip of your soul

I will immortalize your tales

A brave prince's sword

Bathed in enemy's blood

The world will soon overturn

In both fire and flood

A flask of dragon-fire warm

Bluer than the deepest of skies

Trade it for true-love's-kiss spell

From a necromancer's lies

This here, this here

Is a poor man's tale

Written in a book of spells

"How to Raid a Dragon's Lair"

Buy if for a shilling

I will give you a fine deal

Give me an ounce of your emotion

For a witch's last meal

You can buy a brother's undying loyalty

Make you too brave for any fear

But what part of you will you lose...

At the goblin market, here?

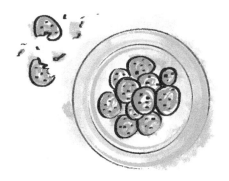

COOKIES FOR GHOST

Clara faces the attic door, armed with a picnic basket and shielded with blankets. She drags a stool into the hallway so her eight-year-old arms can ease the folding ladder out inch by inch without squeaking. The clock on the wall says 1 a.m., far past her bedtime, but this is the only chance she'll get. Daytime is no use.

The attic is dank, smelling of mold and years-old dust. Her parents tried to stick a dehumidifier up here once—it didn't last long. Her father found it taken apart screw by screw and piece by piece, deposited beside the attic's trapdoor. Opening the little window in the far wall only succeeded in it slamming shut later that night. A sliver of moonlight reaches through it. There's the patter of little feet along the grimy wood. Clara hopes they're mice—rats are the worst.

Boxes line the walls, an old armoire looming like a giant opposite the door, leaving space in the center for Clara to spread a blanket and unpack her basket. Out comes the battery-driven lamp her uncle gave her for Christmas, lending a little light to the dark corners. Then the first aid kit from the bathroom.

Tapping starts at the door of the armoire, long pale fingers like candlesticks appearing around the edge. Clara glances down the hallway, where the safety of her room waits, but she can't leave. She likes this new place they've moved to. Her school is nice, and her new friends live down the street. Her room is like a little fortress when she hangs blankets and lights over her bed and chairs, and a forest runs for miles and miles behind the house, unexplored territory for her and her brother.

But no one can get rid of the girl in the attic, so Clara's parents say they're going to move.

That won't happen if Clara can help it. She turns her back on the bright hallway and sits cross-legged on the blanket.

The attic girl pulls herself free of the wardrobe bit by bit, her limbs hitting the floor with a sound like crumpled paper. She's spent nights howling at nothing and terrifying anyone who tries to come near. Clara herself has only seen her once, peeking out the attic trapdoor at her and her brother, yowling when they finally caught sight of her.

The attic ghost crawls towards her like a snake, further tearing her off-white nightdress on the splintery floor. Her dark eyes glare at Clara, fingers reaching, mouth opening with a building howl. Clara winces at the noise sending chills down her spine but plants her hands on her hips.

"Knock that off!" She assumes her best adult voice. "Don't you know yelling at people is rude?"

The screeching stops. Clara listens, but can't hear her parents coming to investigate. It's such a common occurrence no one even gets out of bed anymore.

Ghost blinks at her, ceasing her slow advance. She's drooling a little, and Clara tries not to notice. Not that it bothers her, but staring seems rude. Unpacking the picnic basket, Clara pulls out a carton of milk and some glasses, and the cookies her mother made for tomorrow's school field trip. This seems like a better cause. Ghosts should like chocolate chip, and it's a good excuse for Clara to have a snack in the middle of the night.

She pours a glass of milk and drops in a cookie, setting it out where Ghost can crawl to it.

"Do you want a cookie?"

It's a while before she moves again, but Ghost pushes off her belly and onto her knees, staring sideways at Clara, head resting on her shoulder like she can't hold it up correctly. Cuts bleed from her cheeks and forehead. It renders her a truly horrible sight, but Clara wouldn't want people to fear cuts on her face, so she stays seated and nudges the cookie plate closer.

"What's your name?" she asks.

Ghost stares and makes a noise like a pipe breaking.

"Never mind, I'll bring you a piece of paper tomorrow and you can write it down."

Ghost pouts like a scolded puppy and crawls forward to pick up a cookie. Her hair hangs around her shoulders in stringy knots. She needs a bath terribly after living in the armoire so long. It's drafty up here, the snowy outside air blowing in through cracks around the window. Not enough to clear the air, but enough to make Clara's fingers numb. She peels off one of her blankets, tossing it over Ghost's shoulders. It doesn't float through but sinks in a little, staying mostly on her skin. Ghost jumps at the contact and hisses.

"Be nice," Clara says, and the insubstantial girl blinks apologetically.

She pours more milk and pops open the first aid kit. "I'm going to put some Band-Aids on your face, okay?"

Ghost's skin is not as cold as Clara expects, and she holds nice and still while Clara patches up her cheeks. The bandages don't entirely disappear, but pale against her skin. Satisfied, Clara packs away her things. Ghost hunches over sadly, her lips moving to make some sort of howl.

"Come on," Clara says. "If you promise not to screech at people, you can come haunt my closet. It's got bunches of pillows and it's a lot warmer than your wardrobe."

Ghost bobs her pale head and crawls on her hands and knees down the ladder, silent as a mouse. Clara grins and leads the other girl to her room. She loves to make new friends.

CLOTH LAMB

they've left you in the gnarled
elbow crook of the oak tree

string-worn and lint-beaded
dew baptizing your cotton limbs

you think those rabbits you see
with their yawning teeth, their downy

fur that makes your strings shiver
o, and quiver, in the resting cold twilight

they know nothing, nothing of not being real
of waiting for a child's fingers to remember

to pluck you up again, to dry you by firelight
let you sleep tucked within sheets, within

monsters of white clouds where faerytales are told
and your head, your head is filled with their dreams

GET DOWN

If I'd known there was a truck coming through town, I'd have told my son to get down. Duck behind a road barrier. Slip into the shadows of an alley. Don't go anywhere near those things. But I only see it when a rumbling brings me to the window. It's an army truck without the camouflage, the tarp over the back a drab brown.

A man is perched on the roof of the cab, out in the open, and I feel like shouting across the dreary buildings, ordering him to get down. He grips a handle on the roof for dear life as the vehicle bumps and shifts over the cracked asphalt. He catches me looking from my apartment three stories up, and his expression says *get down*.

I glare daggers, and he jerks his chin away as if he'd never seen me. The truck shudders on. I lean out the window and take a picture with the little camera around my finger. My leg is dangling over the windowsill. I glance at the concrete below and my stomach twists.

Get down off that ledge.

If I'd seen that truck from a distance, I'd have gone looking for my son in the streets. I can imagine him peeking around some empty building or over the top of a garbage bin, and that soldier giving him the same look he'd given me. I've been telling my boy since he was little, but I don't think he would've gotten down.

Humming a lullaby, I open the picture I've taken and sketch it in charcoal on a pad of hard paper. I ran out of paint ages ago.

My son comes in filthy, smudges of dirt or soot or something on his chin and cheeks and round little nose. His eyes are bright, hands behind his back, lip curled in a mischievous way. I snap a picture of that expression so I can draw it later.

"Mom!" he objects, screwing up his face.

I eye his arms. "What do you have there?"

He holds it up. "Fell off that truck."

It's a rusty ball, the size of a large grapefruit, once a shining copper. I bite the insides of my cheeks until I taste iron.

"What is it?"

I smooth his hair, getting a better look at his dirty face. "Years ago, people played games. This ball connected to your thoughts and you could shoot targets at your opponent. If you didn't get down in time, you were out."

If you didn't get down in time, you were dead.

I wander to the kitchen, wetting a towel to wipe the grime from his cheeks. He jumps on the table dramatically, pretending to pitch the orb like a baseball. "Why don't they play those games anymore?"

"People lost interest. Like they eventually do with everything. Get down."

He leaps to the floor. "Can I keep it?"

"For tonight. We'll take it somewhere tomorrow."

I remove it from his hand while his lower lip pouts—the metal cold and caked with corrosion—and set it on the shelf above the sink.

. . .

"Why are we throwing it in the sea?"

"Because," I say, hoisting him onto a rock. The smell of salt and seaweed is kicked up by the breeze. "It's not a good thing for us."

He doesn't understand sentences like that, but one day I may be able to explain it in a way that makes it right. Or at least real.

"The trucks were gathering them all up." He says it like a fact, a question buried beneath.

"They're old and broken now. Broken things like this can be dangerous."

"Did you and Dad play these games?"

I don't join him on the rock. I stand, arms wrapped securely around his legs, smelling the salty air. "Your dad did. A long time ago."

"Did he get down?"

My eyes burn. "No."

My boy picks at the ball, turning it over in his hand. Weighing it like a foreign object, he hurls it into the sea with all his infant might. He sways on the rock as the waves crash below, held tight by my arms. I rest my chin on the stone beside his feet. Red clay fills my nose, tingling my eyes. Ocean spray mists the edge of the boulder.

I take out a drawing of the sphere I made for him, tucking

it into his pocket. He's absorbed in the view, ignoring the dizzying height. I sigh and close my eyes, holding him steady.

When I tell him to get down, he falls safely into my arms.

UNTITLED #2

he could shed his skin
and shear his hair
to form chrysalises
around his soul

so i bathed his
raw flesh in
the ointment of
kisses, twisted his hair
into talismans
around my neck,
and caught salt
in his tears to sing
him wise words of love

THE PETALS ON HER LIPS

The lilies in the spring grew soft and off-white. They grew under leftover snows. Up their buds pushed through ice, glistening in a sun still wintery and pale. When the townsfolk passed by, they stood still, soldiers at attention, and swayed in the breeze. When the witch passed by, they took up their petals and danced.

. . .

She wasn't a witch in the way you and I might think, and it wasn't a name she'd given herself. Her small house was neither dark nor sagging. It stood in the forest under an oak that's branches were so thick it seemed from a distance as if the house and tree were grasping each other for support. The sun filtered down, and her garden had found a happy spot of sunlight. She did not plant lilies, but the village children often left them on her doorstep, thinking of cheering her, and she laid them in the little spring beside her house to soak water into their petals. Passersby thought of it as an old house, an interesting house, not a witch's den.

. . .

It so happened when she was young, as if often does, that there was a boy. He was a blacksmith's son who wanted to be a soldier, and she had only begun to learn the things that would later earn her the title of witch.

The moss in the woods where he waited smelled sweet, and the air warm, or so I'd heard. Lilies grew along the boulders, popping against the dark of the forest like bits of lint on black fabric. They watched the boy, over the edge of the stone, watched the way he shifted his weight, wrung his hands nervously, and craned his neck to look down the path, listening for the sound of her humming.

"Hi, Soldier Boy Bo." She smiled at him when she passed because he was always there when she went from her parents' farm to the clearing in the forest where the lilies grew thickest. He never talked, but this time he caught her elbow and pulled her against the cool stone. He gave her a kiss that half missed her lips and tried to flee before she caught her arm around his neck and kissed him properly.

The lilies on the boulder peeked over the edge and rustled.

. . .

No, witch was not a name she'd given herself, but she didn't mind. It was spoken by those outside the village who didn't know any better but to think an old woman with a feel for magic was something to be wary of. Although she could be found sunken in her porch chair more times than not, silent and not very welcoming of the visitors that traversed her woods, the townsfolk thought of her with fondness.

Her magic had a giving nature, but to her it was quite unkind. How exactly it worked, I can't tell you. People called it everything from curse to blessing and blamed it on everything from the song the wolves howled the night she was born to her parents letting her play barefoot in the forest as a child.

Let us say there were many a man, woman, or child in the village who needed things mended. Not the broken bones or cuts or sicknesses that were all too mendable by doctors. But things that weren't. There was a child born with a foot that wouldn't set straight, wouldn't hold his weight. A man who found himself no longer able to work for his family because his back had bent and tightened. A woman who earned a scar for trying to put out a barn fire, then refused to abandon her room for fear of her lover seeing it.

These were the things she could fix, and for that the villagers came to care for her. She stayed to herself in her little leaning house, but was visited often. They were thankful, and often caring. She helped when it was needed, and came away with a limp, a stooped back, and a puckering scar from eye to chin. And other such things as this.

. . .

The boy she kissed married her when they grew older. It had been years since that kiss when next they met. The blacksmith's son found his sword and his position as a soldier, one in a thousand faces in the army of a small kingdom just over the mountains. He trained three years and served eight, and when he finally found his way home, she was known as both a witch and a lovely young woman. Her body was pockmarked with scars, but she held none of the injuries that would define her later years. She didn't yet have the courage to break herself for others.

He stumbled upon her singing in the clearing of lilies, and wondered at her scars, and if he'd changed in her eyes as much as she'd changed in his. There was something unfair in the way she looked at him and in how beautiful she still was. He thought she didn't recognize him between the years that had passed and the sword on his hip, until she squinted, smirked, and said, "Hi Soldier Boy."

There were dandelion seeds in the air, released by the autumn heat. They clung to her hair, and caught in his eyelashes, making it difficult to see.

"Marry me," he said, not really serious but not really kidding, and most of all not knowing what possessed him.

She laughed and said no, tucked a lily into the twine around his sword handle, and ran back down the path.

A year later, she did anyway.

On their wedding night, he slipped the nightgown from her shoulders and kissed each scar he found.

. . .

His kingdom called him back to war. It had been two dozen years, and he'd built her a little house under a young oak tree. They had no children, for she'd given that ability away years ago to a young woman who'd dreamed of little babies in her arms. It didn't matter to them. With her magic and his war, it seemed the appropriate thing.

That day, he took his sword from the dusty corner, kissed her with a smile, and joked, "I'll be right back."

The day he returned, she buried him in the field of lilies, humming some old, broken tune. The flowers were all dead in the winter frosts, their petals brown and shriveled on the bare ground. They didn't dance and didn't watch her, not in this season.

A mother with a child waited for her, unaware and absorbed in her own worries. She offered the witch the squirming bundle in her arms, chattering, following the witch into her house, crying when she felt she wasn't being heard. The child with a twisted leg, who smiled at the witch over the edge of his blanket, drooling happily. When the witch gathered the warm bundle in her arms, she startled the mother as she wept and broke herself for someone else.

. . .

The witch gathered her scars, her bent back, her bad leg, her twisted lip, her weak fingers, her scars, her scars, her scars. She made the walk to the woods every day and knelt in the lilies, sang to her garden, and let the village children bring her flowers. The oak tree over the house grew and bent itself worse than her. And finally, my mother, after visiting her for years, came with a child of a year old, who the witch healed, and sat down at the end of the day without her sight. She sat in her chair, and tended her garden, but could not make the walk to her husband's grave.

My mother wept at causing the witch this pain.

. . .

As the story is told, the witch walked the path of the woods only once more.

In spring, when it was warm enough for her body not to

ache, she stepped on the familiar route by memory while the lilies took up their petals and danced to show how deeply they'd missed her.

The grave was hidden in grasses and petals, but she wouldn't have seen it anyhow. When the trees parted and she could feel the sun on her cheeks, she knelt and crawled until she found a little stone cross. She sat beside it, and would have sang, but her voice had gone to one of the few travelers she'd helped, for the boy she had given it to sang her most beautiful songs when she'd given it.

The lilies let their petals go, drifting in the air, hands wrapping around her. She lifted her face, and her lips gave him a kiss that mostly missed his own. There was no weight to him, even when the petals touched her lips, and kissed her properly, and surrounded every inch of her. The soldier and the witch swirled, filled the woods, and came to settle across her little house and little garden.

. . .

When my mother made her daily visit, a basket of bread and jam on her arm, her path was carpeted with lilies thicker than the winter snows. Lilies sprouted along the roof, the trees, the stones, and the spaces in the garden, letting their buds fall open, dancing in the breeze. They were everywhere, even in the places she was sure she couldn't see.

And my mother knew just enough of magic to cry as she opened the door, letting the lilies inside breathe.

. . .

I visit her house every now and then, though it's fallen into disrepair. The lilies don't need much tending—the forest keeps them happy and full—but they seem better when I've pulled the crabgrass and thistle from their petals. The flowers whisper and sing in a way no one else seems to hear, other than a young man from the village who once had a bad leg and an older woman who tells stories about putting out a barn fire in her youth. A few others as well, who've made the trek through the lily-strewn woods.

I visit every now and then, to thank her for my sight, and to let her lilies breathe away from the weeds. When I walk the path back home, the flowers like to take up their petals and dance.

UNTITLED #4

when his lies
were no longer
a comfort to
his ragged soul,
i nursed the
truth from his
helpless heart

he choked on
the knives that
spilled from his
tired lips, and
confessed the
only comfort
was in my
forgiveness

PAPER FOUND IN GARDEN,
SECURED WITH LOCKET,
UNBROKEN

One.

Take the locket wrapped round this paper. Cut your finger along its broken edge. It'll serve you well to hold tight along the skin of your neck or the bones in your wrist—tucked inside your cheek will work in a pinch, but be sure to spit it out before you leave. Ensure the hair and grains of sand within have not been stolen by wind and lost to dust. This won't be much use without them.

Please, if the cord it hangs on has rotted to dust, don't bother continuing. It'll be far too late. I am gone and so is the one this is intended for. Carry on, sweet stranger. Bury this. Burn it. Forget.

Two.

The finger bones are in a tin in the back cupboard over the stove. Behind the jars of blackberry preserves. One is mine, yes. It would never have worked with just yours, so calm your frown. Smash them to a dry powder. Do it inside, we don't need the breeze running off with our pain.

Three.

In case some hapless wanderer has decided to continue with these directions, I say to you now that playing with your soul is no trivial matter. Besides, these trinkets won't work for you. Magic is wiser than the best of us.

To my love: steel yourself. I explained this years ago but nothing I could say would have quite covered it. You knew it once but it was so long ago…and leaving your human skin is so different than coming into it. This may be simple but it is not for the weak of heart. *Your* heart will bear it, I know.

Four.

You'll need a rabbit. Alive. Unharmed. You know why. Don't go into the woods. Those are wild and filled with their own magic. One will come to you in the garden if you sit long enough—gray and small with black speckles running down their spines. Speckles are important, like the shade our pear tree made on the sunny yard. Hold her in your hands. Give her a kiss. I am in all of them, so the one you catch…she will be me, and I will remember.

Five.

Take a pear from the tree, squeeze its juice into the bones and mix. (A drop of your blood will do no harm.) If it no longer stands, a cut of the roots will do, beaten into a pulp. Let her lick some from your fingers, she'll stay with you then.

Six.

Take the rest for yourself.

Seven.

If your armor still weighs your shoulders, unburden yourself. Find a place for your sword and your things of war. Mine were left for the trees to grow round. Your clothes will need to go too, now or nearer to the end.

Eight.

Shave those pretty locks of hair. Long fur won't do you much good among the roots and undergrowth.

Nine.

That human skin you took long ago won't be ready to set you free. They're stubborn, they are, like the people in them. There's no need for knives or pain, but find a place to sit where you'll remember. Hold the locket, the pieces of us in it. Hiding them away won't do much good, but you need to let them go. Let all of it go.

Ten.

Remember the first day we met, the way the trees bloomed and the awkward slope of your smile. The way it felt to meet another like ourselves.

Remember the last day. How we held one another. It seemed the warmth of your arms would stay burned into my skin for the rest of our years. The weight of your sword that for so long had been nimble and unburdened. We swore on the sky and the trees and the waters we'd find our way back to one another.

Remember until it hurts.

Eleven.

I love you. I'm here. Hold me tight, I'll see you in a moment.

Note.

And if, by chance, this locket happens to be unbroken: stranger, you needn't worry. The magic has finished its work.

Watch the rabbits in the garden—gray with dark speckles—they're wiser than they appear.

Do not bury or burn this.

Leave it be, smile, and forget.

WATCHMEN

something in the way
your house watches the hills where
the trees pray and the coyotes play watchmen
paws in the topsoil tails beating like war drums
and eyes eyes eyes over the sticker-grasses
vigilant and moonbeam-dipped
makes it almost seem like a real thing again
less of a fog-whisper and more like birdsong

ALL THE WOODS SHE WATCHES OVER

The wolf arrives the same day Adeline buries Hugo on the edge of the woods, her boy's grave forming a raft of upturned earth between two trees, just far enough from the fens that he won't be drowning. She watches two young village men blanket him in icy soil. His shotgun leans against a nearby tree. His hunting knife is tucked under her shirt, against her back. Bone handle followed by colder steel. A second spine to hold her upright.

Behind her, the villagers' thoughts cover her like a summer heat, so oppressive and consistent she drowns in it. *Bears, bears, bears. In winter. Bears.*

Her daughter-in-law, Irene, seems to wither under the unspoken worry, all the eyes on her and Adeline's grand-daughter. Adeline touches the other woman's hand but doesn't speak—they've never been close—and thinks vaguely of wolves. The pressure of their paws on the undergrowth. The heat of their breath. She hums Hugo's name silently in the back of her throat and holds her granddaughter like a shield before her.

There is a wisp of fur in the long shadows of evening that follows her home.

. . .

Her house is not much like her own grandmother's, but there are several oaks hemming it like old giants. She cracks the window to her bedroom, letting leaves and the occasional leftover acorns find their way onto her floor. Winter air creeps in. She doesn't sleep. Her body is cold stone under the covers, her face feeling liable to crack.

Some of Hugo's things are packed between the night-table and bedpost, smelling of pine, sharp and sure. His coat, she has laid across her chest. Like cracked mud or dying bark, a shield of brown fabric against the night. Adeline concentrates on crying and can't manage it.

When she smells the creature outside, she turns her face into her pillow and refuses to acknowledge the fact that there are paws and teeth and the heady scent of the woods on the other end of the door. Her granddaughter is a mile out of the trees, nearer to town. She hardly knows the girl, and her mother even less. Hugo left these woods for a time, returning with a woman foreign but kind, a daughter in his arms. Adeline loves the child, but hardly knows her granddaughter's eyes.

Her husband is in the dirt, as her son is now. The house feels quiet, though it's sheltered only her for years.

Does her granddaughter sleep? There must be many village men awake and on guard against the winter bear that took Hugo. Rifles across their knees, coffee warming their bellies. She must be safe. Adeline wonders if the little girl feels the other, not-quite-here things in the woods.

There are paws on her doorstep. This she knows rather than

hears, and knows it until she peels back the blankets and puts her bare feet on the wooden floor. Quiet as can be managed, she puts a match to the lantern and lifts the latch on the door. A halo of light cuts across the porch. She doesn't wish to look long at the illuminated beast waiting for her. She is alone, but not in need of company. Words stick in her throat for too long

"Come to tell me my boy's dead, you're a day too late." Her voice cracks. "Buried him in your woods."

The wolf is quite larger than the ones that roam in packs, thinking of hunger, hunger, the trees, and sometimes the moon and her stars. They are indifferent to men and women, take only spare moments here and there to be curious of children. They are not this. This reminds her of her childhood. The hands of her grandmother. The whisper of a new cloak around her ankles. Teeth. A hunter's ax.

Hunter. *Hugo.* Adeline shakes herself.

She wishes to close the door. Hugo's shotgun is beside her own at the door. Her limbs protest sudden movements and long walks these days, her eyes don't like the dark, but her hands know the work of the weapon. Deep down, she knows the shotgun isn't needed. This is not *that* wolf. This one whines at her words, for however much wolves understand grief. This is an old friend, but Adeline's son is dead, and she has no time for the worries of wolves and bears, for the quarrels that foxes start with badgers. The world doesn't have much time for these kinds of faerytales any more.

But the whine starts an ache in her chest. You don't send someone away into the winter woods. Shame over the thought of casting the wolf out mixes with the guilt of ever letting her son set foot between the trees. She lets the door fall open.

He finds the woodstove humming with coals and settles.

Mud and bits of leaves are left where his paws fall. His winter coat is matted, and Adeline wants to pick the twigs from it. She approaches slowly, taking a wide loop to the side so he sees her before sidling closer and putting water on the stove to boil. Kicking a pillow closer, she sets herself down. The flame from her lamp and glow of the coals through the cracks of the stove's door fills the house with ghosts.

"I watched you bury him," the wolf says, and Adeline finds that a strange comfort.

"Thank you," she says. Wolves don't much bother to care for human problems. Not even the one warming himself by her fire.

She leans close enough to stoke the fire back to life. Bitter copper fills her nose, strong enough she can taste it on the back of her tongue. Too much blood today. First, her son's. Now something she can't make out in the darkness. She leaves his side long enough to splash her face with water and return with the lamp and clean cloths.

"What happened?"

"I knew a lark that befriended a hawk once. A storm came in spring so bitter and sudden the lark's eggs froze in her nest—"

"Must it be a grieving story tonight, wolf?"

She has no name for him she can speak. She knows him like a familiar smell or an ache of recognition, the same way she knows when winter has started. Any time she's asked for a name, he tells her a story. Sometimes she can peel them apart, find some meaning at the core. Many times, they're gibberish.

"You are a grieving story tonight, Adeline."

Her throat burns for a moment so brief she isn't sure it's real pain. So carefully it's hardly even a touch, she brushes her fingers against the edge of his hind leg. The fur is coarse.

Heat from his skin makes her cold fingers tingle back to life. The growl in his chest seems automatic, for he lays his head down and keeps his peace the next time she tries. Something has gouged the flesh around his ribs. The shape of the wound is suspiciously tooth-like. Large-jawed.

Bear, she thinks again, suddenly certain of her diagnosis.

It's been too long since she's been to the village—she cuts away fur and does her best with what her garden provides. The whole place smells of herbs and oils.

"Once the bear king came out of his winter sleep still tired," the wolf says; Adeline starts when she hears the word out loud. "He could not hunt nor scavenge and grew more and more ill over the hot days of summer. He slept early in autumn and never woke. Miles away, a new cub was born to take his place. But she was a tiny little thing in her mother's paws. When one of her kind went mad in the snows, she was not yet old and strong enough to protect her woods."

They are quiet for longer than Adeline can count. "I think that was the most straightforward thing you've ever spoken."

"The bear…"

"It will be killed."

"You're sure of that?"

She isn't, and her silence speaks to her doubt.

"I am too old for a mad bear, Little Red."

Adeline puts her hand under his armpit, against his chest bone where his heartbeat taps against her palm like a mothwing. She knows enough of wolves and their panting breaths and hot quick blood to feel dull worry at the slowness of it. Today's loss has left her nerves splintered, and she feels the weight of the late night. Though the wound is large, it is not deep. This is a sickening Adeline does not understand. Has the entire world fallen to it? She thinks it must have, in this winter where her village is afraid, her son is dead, and her friend...

"That's not my name," she says, an old argument. "And I'm too old for you to be dying on my floor, wolf."

He blinks lazily at the light of the stove, and Adeline throws a blanket over him despite the trouble he's brought her way.

"There was once what you humans would call a king in his castle—"

Adeline bolts the door for the first time since she was a child, draws every curtain, and curls before the fire like a wolf pup against her old friend.

. . .

A thing for certain Adeline knows about wolves: They are mostly not dishonest.

People are quite the opposite, she's found. Most lie. Sometimes, you'll find one so honest it hurts. It's almost laughable that the first wolf she met was intent on deception. He was friendly. Liked the red of the cloak her grandmother made her and wanted to meet the woman. Adeline had been dreaming of wolves since she toddled about on baby legs trying to make friends with the moths and scarecrows. She dreamed of the wolves' hunting and their eyes. The sharpness of their noses and slopes of their tails. This wolf walked beside her, and she could listen to the otherworldly rasp of his voice as he told her how much he favored the cakes she was bringing to her grandmother.

Later, she figured he liked the cloak not at all, or because it was the color of blood. She knew afterward why he wanted to meet her grandmother.

She saw the *other* wolf—not the silver-tongued one back in her grandmother's cottage split down the belly like a fish—while she was behind the outhouse, retching up everything she'd ever eaten. He had the strangest expression. Eyes far too large. Human. She was ready to scream when he ducked his head and stepped away non-threateningly.

"I am sorry." His voice sounded like he wasn't used to speaking. He trotted to the side of the house, his nose touching the window frame before he slunk back into the trees.

She saw the hunter hauling the carcass of the creature that had almost eaten her whole.

Her mother forbade her from venturing into the trees after that, and her grandmother came to stay with them for a time. That very night she'd slipped out the window in her nightgown. The village sat in an opening in the woods, miles and miles of trees beginning a dozen yards from her parents' house. It was spring. Heavy dew hung from the grass, wetting her toes and the hems of her gown. The moon was full, and she wanted to howl at it. When she found the wolf lying at the edge of the trees, she sat on a fallen trunk nearby.

"Are you a faerytale?" she asked. *A dream?*

"No."

"Why did you apologize to me?"

"Because I protect my kind. And I take care that they do no wrong," he said, and told her a story about the animals he befriends, the woods he watches over, and the way the trees arrange themselves.

When she was much older, Adeline taught her son to always beware wolves, but never to hunt them.

. . .

A rattling on the door wakes her. The fire has died. The kettle atop the stove is stone cold. Warmth seeps into her skin from the wolf's snout resting on the side of her waist, but she's cold down to the bone. She puts a hand on the floor. Her hips, knees, shoulder, neck, even her ankles ache from sleeping on wood. Age does not suit her.

A knock follows the rattling. "Grandma? It's Fern. Are you there?"

The little girl's voice is solemn, and Adeline is half awake but vaguely angry. Surely Irene is here as well, but they should *not* be here, walking through the woods in the morning light with a starving, rabid bear hunting for all the food it can get.

She glances at the creature beside her, his dark eyes staring unblinking. People are not so ready to believe in magic as they once were. There aren't many around who will remember a time when you could strike a friendship with a wolf.

"Go into my bedroom," she says. "In the closet in the back."

She rises with some difficulty and unbolts the door. The air outside is an icy wave, slithering through her thin nightgown and the blanket over her shoulders. Snow floats on the breezes like scraps of tissue paper, taking their time to disappear onto the ground. The beginnings of an approaching storm. Six-year-old Fern chews on her littlest gloved finger and blinks up at her. Irene stands down off the porch with Albert, one of the bigger young men in the village. A shotgun is slung across his shoulder, and Adeline nods at him approvingly. Irene is not as foolish as Adeline's sleeping mind imagined. She pulls Fern against her, covering her shoulders in the blanket she wears. The girl wriggles a bit but doesn't pull free.

"Everything well, Irene?"

Her daughter-in-law looks like she hasn't slept an hour this last night. Her eyes are dim, skin dull, shoulders bent. She wrings her hands around the handle of the basket of food she's brought. Adeline figures her own face probably looks as drawn.

"We think you should come stay with us a while, Mama. At least until that..." —the word catches in her throat, and she visibly glances into the trees— "*monster* creature is caught."

Adeline used to bristle against the girl saying the motherly name, but it made Hugo smile, and she's lost any will to keep up those thoughts. Irene isn't quite ready to live amongst the trees, but she's a good girl. She loved Hugo. Instead, Adeline imagines Hugo's grin whenever it happened, the one tooth on the top row of teeth shorter than the rest.

When Adeline's grandmother came to live with them, leaving her little cottage in the woods, she never went back. She spent every day with them, and although Adeline cherished having the woman closer, she didn't fail to notice the way she stared into the trees, how the animals of her mother's garden came to her, but she never really went back home. Adeline might be able to stand it—never walking these paths again, never sleeping with the eyes of the forest just outside her wall—but this is where Hugo grew up. And she has a friend to care for.

"I'm all right, girl. I don't go out much in this weather anyhow."

Irene sucks her top lip in between her teeth, eyes trailing after Fern as she wanders Adeline's porch. "You're sure nothing'll happen to you? You won't go outside if you think anything's out there?"

Adeline smiles a little. The movement cracks her face as if she hasn't done it in ages. "I can keep myself to myself. I promise."

Irene nods and sets the basket on the top step of the porch. Adeline is reluctant to leave the door, but steps forward to take it, genuine gratitude curling in her chest. She doesn't need the provisions, but the younger woman means well. For the little time they've spent together, it's more than she expected.

"You should get on back before this blizzard rolls in. It gets colder than anyone's business out here in the winter." She looks at Albert and manages to keep her voice level. "Anyone see that bear?"

She doesn't miss the slightest downturn of his mouth, the pull-together of his eyebrows. "Markus thought he saw something last night on the edge of the woods. Huge. Shaped like a bear. But he filled it with enough lead to kill ten bears and it disappeared. Figures it must have been a shadow. Nothing would live through that."

Adeline swallows thickly, a strange sensation rolling her stomach. Do they truly believe it was a shadow? Albert's jaw works, his eyes on his boots or the trees. He's frightened, and Adeline feels she should be as well. Instead, the dull ache that started last night in her chest becomes a pounding thing with teeth and claws. She feels sick. She wants to know what faerytale out there killed her boy and sheds bullets.

"Mama?" Fern drapes herself over the porch railing. "Did Papa hunt bears?"

Irene makes a noise like someone's punched her, quiet and low in her throat.

"Yes," Adeline says gently, half-hearing her own words. "And it was a foolish thing he did."

Fern blinks up at her, her eyes drifting down through the crack in the door and widening. When Adeline glances back, she sees her wolf still slumped by the stove, his head propped up against the leg of a chair, watching them. Her mouth opens with some half-formed explanation, but Fern only stares at her in wonder, a smile tugging at the corner of her mouth. She lets her grandmother steer her back down the steps to Irene.

"I'll come by when the storm has calmed. With a present for you."

"For me?" Fern grins enough to show the gaps in her baby teeth.

"Just for you."

Irene looks like she's trying to smile but can't quite manage it. She takes her daughter into her arms. Adeline touches her shoulder. A pitiful comfort.

"Albert?" she says after they've turned away. The young man looks over his shoulder. "If any of you see that bear, shoot it, but don't get anywhere close to it."

He frowns but nods, glancing from side to side all the way down the path until the woods swallow them. They know not to stray, and to walk with quick steps.

Inside, she tells her wolf, "That was a foolish thing to do. I told you to hide."

He lays his head down, whining once, unmoving under the weight of whatever ails him. It is quite possible he cannot get up. Quiet fills the house. Adeline itches in her skin, almost ready to shuck it off and run for the mountains far from here, where men and women do not exist and the forest is a thing without shape or meaning. She imagines the toenails sprouting from her fingertips, the thinning silver hair on her head becoming thick and short, enveloping her like a coat.

Her wolf is still watching her. "Why do you think those things, Little Red?"

His voice is a touch of wind, raspy and hardly-there. Adeline takes a few creeping steps forward, brushing her fingers along the top of his snout. He can't know her strange dreams. Not really.

"What things?" she asks without thought.

She drags on a heavy coat and brings firewood in, slowly, pieces at a time, covering the outside pile with an old tarp. The snow sticks to the ground now, throwing a layer of dirty white across the world. Her house warms slowly. She heats gruel for herself and feeds him bits of salted pork she softens in hot water.

"What gift?" he asks.

Adeline stares at him evenly. His wound is not all that severe, just as she thought, and she feels a strange bitterness at him coming here to die for a reason she can't understand. She feels small and old. Unequal to the task. The resentment fills her with shame.

"The gift for your granddaughter," he clarifies. "You said you're giving her a gift."

There is a chest under her bed filled with many things. Hugo's baby shoes. Her husband's wedding ring. Black and white photos so grainy only she really knows the faces on them. Adeline pulls a length of thick red wool from its depths. She unclasps the front of the cloak and puts her face against the rough fabric. It hasn't been around her shoulders in decades, but smells of pine and soil nonetheless.

"I remember that," he says when she's taken a seat in the chair beside the stove. She pulls out her sewing things and begins hemming the length of the wool, bringing in the shoulders and making the hood smaller. When she's grown, Fern can cut the threads and make it long once again.

"Tell me why you weren't frightened that day you saw me."

Adeline doesn't expect the question—he doesn't usually ask them. "I don't know. I'd been sneaking into the forest and trying to talk to the animals my entire life. And I was frightened of you, I just wasn't quite ready to give up on whatever magic I thought I saw. Tell me how you became who you are."

She expects a story, but receives a very straightforward, "The same way anyone becomes the way they are: They're born."

"Is that all?" A disappointment she can't understand overtakes the worry in her chest for only a moment.

"What more did you want?"

Something beautiful and believable, she supposes. Or horrible and believable.

"I was born before there were war-planes in the sky and the trees became parted by trains. There was a boy I knew once who was much like you. He talked to flowers and sought time with the animals though he was still very small."

He pauses long enough she asks, "What happened to him?"

"He found a dying badger. She told him he could dance with them. Become one with the dirt and the worms and the heartbeat of the woods. When she died, he took her skin upon him and ran with badger feet through the world."

"Did he ever return?"

"He would visit his family, but only his sister could see him as the little brother she held dear."

Adeline pulls out a crooked stitch. "And you've come here to die on me as well? Like my husband and my son?"

Grief is a tangible thing sometimes. She can hear it in his breathing, see it in the way his face crinkles around his eyes. Maybe wolves are better at heartache than she thought. The stitches she makes in her granddaughter's cloak begin to blur, and Adeline thinks this is not what should be making her cry, even if they aren't real tears yet.

Her wolf lays his head on her feet and sleeps.

. . .

Hugo was four years old when Adeline first took him deep enough into the woods that the only paths were the kind made by the paws of animals. The whole place smelled of summer heat, the soil hot and baking where the sun cut through the trees, her tongue heavy with the scent of pine sap. Hugo ran ahead and jumped from every fallen log while her husband, Paul, held her hand. He was a carpenter and a good man, quiet and stable. Even without fully understanding her relationship with the trees and the creatures in them, he accepted what she knew and didn't question the way she knew it.

He'd met her wolf years ago, and although he wouldn't speak to the creature, Paul let him eat from his hand, and his eyes held only curiosity. When she wanted Hugo to meet the wolf, she was answered with a smile.

"Mama, where are we going?"

"To meet a friend, little bird."

"Out *here?*"

"Indeed," she said, and her husband chuckled.

They didn't find one another in any particular way. Adeline knew that if she walked enough, he'd eventually find their path.

"Mama, a wolf!" Hugo's voice was a whisper anyone could hear.

She took Hugo by the hand and pulled him onto a log so that he was eye to eye with the creature. Her wolf looked curious, and vaguely amused. He snuffled Hugo's mussed hair and loped through the trees while her boy chased the matted fur of his tail. Hugo was too young to understand what he was experiencing, his giggles echoing off the canopy of the woods. Beside her, her husband laughed and laughed at their boy's wonder.

. . .

It attacks someone else.

When the storm has blown itself out, Adeline maneuvers her wolf onto a blanket and drags him into her bedroom with more than a little difficulty. Tucking him into the corner where no one is likely to look, she leaves a pan of water and throws another quilt across him. He slept through most of the storm but licks her hand as she prepares to leave, and she kneels by his head to stroke his ears.

"Do you fear walking that path alone?" His eyes are heavy-lidded.

"No." She doesn't feel that's the right answer. "Fear and I aren't cooperating since Hu..."

She chokes on his name and her wolf does not push. "Will bullets even do us any good?"

He sighs long and slow, like the air won't leave his lungs. "I don't know. It has a touch of magic same as you and I. And I... I wasn't ready to be fighting it."

There is a despair in his voice so deep it matches the ache in her own chest. She kisses the corner of his eye and walks the path with Hugo's shotgun under her arm, her granddaughter's new cloak tucked into her coat.

Frigid air still rustles the trees, but no snow blinds her way, and the path is free of any life.

The village spreads before her like the forest taking a breath, but she sees a group clustered at the entrance of one of the cottages. Not Hugo's. Not Irene's and Fern's, but Adeline feels something lodge in her throat. She's known the faces of the people around her all her life, feels their concerned eyes on her as she squeezes through the throng to get to the nearest window. Albert sits at the table, his disfigured arm being cleaned by the doctor. Adeline looks away.

"Mama, Mama, Adeline." Irene's fingers wrap around her upper arm, leading her from the window. Her eyes are red.

"What happened?"

"It—the bear came into the village. Albert shot it right in the head but it ran off like it wasn't nothing, good God. Did you walk here by yourself?"

Adeline nods half-heartedly, allowing the younger woman to lead her back to the house Hugo just built for them. Fern blinks at her from the kitchen table but jumps to her feet when her grandmother opens her arms. She puts her face in the girl's hair and breathes, her scent something like Hugo's but not quite.

"I have something for you," she says quietly, unfolding the blood-red cloak from her coat. Fern's mouth forms a little O as Adeline drapes it around her shoulders. "Keep it on when you go into the woods. My grandmother made it for me, and I changed it to fit you."

"It looks like poppies," she says, enamored of the little brass button used to clasp it in the front. Adeline likes that imagery more than anything she could come up with.

She kisses the girl and puts her lips beside her ear. "It'll be over soon. No need to be afraid. I love you, little bird."

She is aware of Irene watching them the way one feels the eyes of animals in the woods, curious and knowing at once.

Her daughter-in-law follows her outside, where she left the shotgun leaning against the wall in the flowerbed.

"You can't walk back alone." She pauses like she knows her own words aren't right and tries again. "What are you going to do?"

Her voice shakes like pine needles in the breeze, her hand at her neck, lower lip unsteady. Adeline thinks of her wolf taking his last breaths in her house, and of the little boy that danced with a badger's skin until he became one. Wolf's magic is old; only Adeline's body is.

She hugs Irene, taking her skinny shoulders into her arms until the girl cries. She gives her a kiss on the forehead same as she gave to her granddaughter. Her throat begins to burn, and doesn't stop as she takes the path back home.

It growls when she reaches her porch: the creature behind her. The bear is large, but not much more so than her wolf. It's ragged and ghost-thin, unlike anything she's ever seen. Pale fur blotches its skin, the roar it makes when it steps forward alien and strange. Adeline fires three shots, backing up the steps into her doorway, sobbing like a madwoman. The bear snarls and flinches from the bullets long enough for her to bolt the door behind her. She can hear its paws on the porch, claws against the door, but her house stands strong and proud as the day it was built, and Adeline lets her son's rifle lean against the wall.

Her wolf is where she left him, breathing deep, too-slow breaths. His eyes watch her through exhausted slits.

Despite the soreness from the other night slept on the floor, she curls around him, weeping into his fur.

. . .

EMILY MCCOSH

"This is not a story, not really," her wolf tells her, his breath on the inside of her palm. "You are not the only friend I've had, but perhaps the best. I know when I'm ready to be in the earth. Your boy crossed my path as I came to find you. He saw my weakness and carried me. The bear crossed our path, and I could not help him fight it."

The night is quiet, and Adeline's body is unmovable, as if the weight of her tears and their shared grief is something to be felt and wrapped around her. She's not released him from her embrace.

"I know what you'll do," he says, soft as the night. "For your granddaughter. I think it's good. I did not tell you that the boy who danced in the badger's skin heard her voice within his heart until he, too, laid down into the earth."

Relief is a breath of air that finally reaches her lungs, a sharp knife against her sorrow. "Good."

He whimpers softer than a breeze, kissing her fingers with a weak tongue.

"You were there with him?" she asks.

"Forgive me for my weakness."

Adeline's arms form a vise around him, her face in the rough fur of his neck, "Always, wolf."

. . .

His pelt comes off like air, solid and musky in her hands. Nothing awaits under the skin but bones that dry and crumble the moment air touches them. Adeline wonders if this is what she will look like inside once the deed is done, and weeps through the task, though his heartbeat has long faded.

On the bed are Hugo's things, and a few other treasures she

· 130 ·

doesn't want lost to time. Irene will find them soon enough.

She sheds her clothes in the cold, cold night, opening every window, breathing out Hugo's name and kissing goodbye the world he knew.

She wraps her new skin around her. For many minutes the wolf is nothing but a wet, warm fur around her old flesh. But she feels it like a birdsong far off, a little pinch in her chest that fails to hurt but leaves her on her knees nonetheless. Salt from her tears mixes with the bloody skin. The walls of her house become confining and narrow, and she slips out the window on four large paws that guide her through the trees, muscles crawling along her back and legs and neck, itching to be used. Her heart pounds like heavy wheels on a train track. A thousand smells fight for her attention. Her tail brushes the back of her legs.

Focus, something inside her says, and a yip of bitter joy at the familiar voice breaks apart her chest.

She smells the bear by the village, all madness and maggot-filled meat. Like a dream, a shadow under the moon, she lopes away from her human home.

. . .

In the spring, Adeline's granddaughter finds a wolf on the edge of the trees. The girl wears her grandmother's poppy-red cloak, and the wolf's dark fur is veined with silver. She remembers the mad bear that took her Papa in the winter, and the wolf that came to drive it away.

She grins with half her baby teeth.

The wolf whines and licks the girl's giggling cheek. Her mother hangs laundry a ways away, and watches with eyes that don't see or don't fear the creature kissing her daughter's neck.

"Grandma," the little girl says.

The wolf settles around her granddaughter and tells her a story of a badger that was once a boy, an old wolf that befriended a young woman, and all the woods she watches over.

THANK YOU FOR READING!

Thank you so much for reading *All the Woods She Watches Over*!

If you would like to support the author and help readers, please consider leaving a review on Amazon, Goodreads, or any other platform of your choice!

ACKNOWLEDGMENTS

As I'm sitting down to write the acknowledgments for my first book, I'm certain I'll never thank all the people I need to thank. Gratitude is slippery like that. Here goes nothing…

First and foremost, to my parents for being the best ever in so many ways. Among other things, to my Mom for being my best friend, listening to all my insane ideas and ramblings about the publishing industry, and for reading all my work. And to my Dad, for being hilarious, clever, and for first telling me, "hey, you should write that book you've been thinking about."

There are a ton of authors who have inspired me in a million little ways: All the lovely people on Authortube making writing videos and giving fantastic publishing advice, and everyone on the Codex Writers Group who have run writing contests and been adorable and encouraging.

And a final thank you to my beta readers, my fabulous and talented editor Natalia Leigh for whipping my book into shape, and Deborah Davitt for being an awesome writer buddy.

ABOUT THE AUTHOR

Emily McCosh is a graphic designer, writer of strange things, and daydreamer extraordinaire. She currently lives in California with her two parents, two dogs, one fish, one tree swing, and innumerable characters who need to learn some manners. Her fiction has appeared in *Beneath Ceaseless Skies, Shimmer Magazine, Galaxy's Edge, Flash Fiction Online, Nature: Futures,* and elsewhere.

Find her online on her writing and bookish YouTube channel, website where she sometimes blogs, and Instagram full of sappy poetry.

YouTube: Emily McCosh

TikTok: emilymccosh

Instagram: emily_mccosh

Blog: oceansinthesky.com

Facebook & Twitter: @wordweaveremily

PUBLICATION HISTORY

"Breath, Weeping Wind, Death" – *Galaxy's Edge* (2019)

"The Stars and the Rain" – *Flash Fiction Online* (2017)

"Of Water and Wood" – *Galaxy's Edge* (2017)

"Frozen Meadow, Shining Sun" – *Beneath Ceaseless Skies* (2018)
        – reprinted at *Flame Tree Press: Epic Fantasy Anthology* (2019)

"Cookies for Ghost" – *Daily Science Fiction* (2019)

"All the Woods She Watches Over" – *Shimmer Magazine* (2018)
                – originally printed as "Rotkäppchen"

Made in the USA
Las Vegas, NV
08 March 2021